The Secretaries

by The Five Lesbian Brothers
Maureen Angelos, Babs Davy,
Dominique Dibbell,
Peg Healey and Lisa Kron

A SAMUEL FRENCH ACTING EDITION

SAMUEL
FRENCH
FOUNDED 1830

SAMUELFRENCH.COM

ISBN 978-0-573-69701-2   Printed in U.S.A.   #29100

MUSIC USE NOTE

IMPORTANT BILLING AND CREDIT
REQUIREMENTS

THE SECRETARIES was first produced at the WOW Café in New York City in December of 1993, under the direction of Kate Stafford. The sets were designed by Amy Shock, costume design was by Susan Young, lighting was designed by Lori E. Seid, sound was designed by Peg Healey and props were designed by Sharon Hayes, who was the stage manager.

This production of the play was also presented at Theatre Rhinoceros, San Francisco; Highways, Los Angeles; Alice B. Theatre, Seattle and DiverseWorks, Houston.

THE SECRETARIES was produced in the version printed here at New York Theatre Workshop, New York City. It opened on September 8, 1994, under the direction of Kate Stafford. Set design was by James Schuette, costume design was by Susan Young, lighting was designed by Nancy Schertler, sound was designed by Darron L. West, the fight director was J. Allen Suddeth, the dramaturg was Sybille Pearson, the production stage manager was Janet M. Clark and the production manager was Susan R. White. The cast was as follows:

DAWN MIDNIGHT/BUZZ BENIKEE	Maureen Angelos
ASHLEY ELIZABETH FRATANGELLO	Babs Davy
PATTY JOHNSON	Dominique Dibbell
SUSAN CURTIS/SANDY/	
MR. RON KEMBUNKSCHER	Peg Healey
PEACHES MARTIN/HANK	Lisa Kron

CHARACTERS

DAWN MIDNIGHT – office lesbian.

ASHLEY ELIZABETH FRATANGELO – Susan's sycophant, bulimic.

PATTY JOHNSON – the new girl.

SUSAN CURTIS – office manager/cult leader.

PEACHES MARTIN – sweet, clueless, slow-moving target.

BUZZ BENIKEE – sensitive lumberjack.

HANK AND SANDY – sexually harassing lumberjacks (slow).

MR. RON KEMBUNKSCHER – the boss.

TIME AND PLACE

The play takes place in and around the town of Big Bone, Oregon.
Some time before Windows '95.

Prologue - Cooney Lumber Mill.
Scene One - The Office.
Scene Two - The Breezy Barn.
Scene Three - The Loading Dock.
Scene Four - Back in the Office.
Scene Five - The Video Store.
Scene Six - The Chorus.
Scene Seven - First Club Meeting.
Scene Eight - Patty and Buzz at the Loading Dock.
Scene Nine - Patty and Peaches in the Bathroom.
Scene Ten - HHH Health and Beauty Night.
Scene Eleven - The Chorus.
Scene Twelve - Back in the Office.
Scene Thirteen - Patty and Buzz on the Phone.
Scene Fourteen - Patty and Dawn at the HHH.
Scene Fifteen - Patty and Dawn: The Morning After.
Scene Sixteen - Susan and Dawn.
Scene Seventeen - In the Car.
Scene Eighteen - Shit Hits the Fan.
Scene Nineteen - Guts/Prep.
Scene Twenty - Kill Night.

AUTHORS' NOTES

BABS DAVY: We wanted to write a musical and Moe had seen a version of *Seven Brides for Seven Brothers* at the Edinburgh Festival that year and was smitten with it. We would play lumberjacks and turn the story on its ear. We rented the movie and were horrified by what we saw: the glorification of rape in song and dance. The men were "doin' what comes nat'rally" and the women would come to like it in the end when they saw what a cool house they could have. We went on retreat to New Hampshire and began writing about lumberjacks and doing improvs about church suppers and pancake breakfasts. We had the shy lumberjack, the singing lumberjack, the mean lumberjack. We put them on the mountain, in the smokehouse, at the restaurant with a terrace overlooking the valley, and in the office where their brides worked at the lumber mill. Nothing happened in these improvs because we had no idea what lumberjacks did aside from yell timber and dance on logs like they did in the movie. We wanted to kill these guys. Dominique had just been reading somewhere about motorcycle girl gangs who kill and torture men for sport. Everyone's face lit up and much excitement and animated discussion in the group commenced. Now we were getting somewhere. Fuck the lumberjacks. We would play the "brides" in the office at the lumber mill.

DOMINIQUE DIBBELL: Something about the brilliant fall colors and piney smell all around us encouraged us to hold onto the idea of lumberjacks. Lisa kept pushing for the introduction of the secretaries who worked at the lumber mill, and eventually we gave them a try. Almost immediately we saw that we had found the vehicle for our simmering anger. Sick and disgusting scenes of the ravages of internalized sexism came pouring forth. We were relieved beyond words that we finally found the play we were already booked to perform in a few months. Lisa summed up our feelings when she impulsively scribbled on her writing pad, then held up for all to see à la *Norma Rae*, the words, "Writing Itself!"

PEG HEALEY: I think this was the first time we consciously used our writing to deal with our dynamic in working together. I remember it was a time when we were worried that Lisa might be leaving the Brothers (actually, aren't we always worried that someone is leaving), but we took that fear and turned it around and decided to analyze what happens when someone new comes into a tight-knit group…and Patty Johnson was born. Susan Curtis was born when Dominique was being interrogated as an improv exercise. Ashley Elizabeth Fratangello was an homage to Elizabeth Ashley. We were obsessed with her SlimFast campaign at the time. Needless to say it permeates the script.

LISA KRON: The play examines the ways in which women are the enforcers of sexism. The rules that are enforced involve weight, food, sexuality. Proof that we were covering uncharted territory was in the disconnect between the responses of men (notably male reviewers) and women. Women recognized what we were doing because they had experienced it. Men did not because they had never seen it before, never had it described to them. Male viewers often focused on the cartoonish violence at the end of the play when poor Buzz is killed with his own chainsaw. The emotional violence between the women did not show up on their radar. They tended to see the play as a revenge fantasy, which it clearly is not. The only likeable character in the play is Buzz and before his bloody execution Susan Curtis makes clear he does not deserve to die: "We don't kill them because they're bad. We kill them because we're bad."

DOMINIQUE DIBBELL: *The Secretaries* gave us our first walkouts. We empathized. Some of us almost walked out of the writing process, too. Confronting issues of body image and woman's cruelty to woman was no picnic. We had many an angst-filled check-in in which we worried that we were promoting violence and/or betraying the feminist movement. But, in the end, our soul-searching made us more passionately devoted to the play. New Yorkers, of course, loved it. They like it in Houston, too, where gun laws are less restrictive.

MAUREEN ANGELOS: *The Secretaries* is a true product of pure collaboration. It is our most artistically successful play, so far; it's the most well constructed. We really stuck to plot with the help of our wise dramaturg Sybille Pearson. It has been the most satisfying process for us.

Prologue
Cooney Lumber Mill

(Lights go dark as a sound cue comes up of chainsaws, which turns into the sound of a man screaming, which turns into the sound of secretaries laughing, which turns into the sound of secretaries clicking and giggling, which turns into the sound of keyboards clicking. [Note: "clicking and giggling" refers to a secret secretarial language made up of rapid chipmunk-like clicking, sucking and popping sounds made with the tongue, intermingled with giggling.] Lights up on the office. On the wall is a calendar which reads: COONEY LUMBER MILL IS PROUD OF 28 ACCIDENT-FREE DAYS. DAWN, ASHLEY, PATTY and PEACHES are at their desks. They type rhythmically while they chant.)

ALL. Enter, enter, enter, enter
Save
Type and type and type and type and type and type and type and type and type.

We welcome you to Big Bone
To share with you our story
We'd like to warn you from the top it gets a little gory.

DAWN. *(spoken, not in rhythm)* Shit! My nail!

ALL. We are secretaries
Like we always dreamed we'd be
We get to wear nice clothes and we get paid a salary.

ASHLEY. *(spoken, not in rhythm)* I'm done with this.

ALL. Ninety words a minute
A hairdo that would stop a truck
Two weeks paid vacation
Sincerely, Mr. Kembunkscher. *(All giggle and click.)*

9

ASHLEY. *(spoken, not in rhythm)* Hey!

ALL. We are a clique

   We type and click

   We type and giggle and click.

   We copy, fax and type real quick

   Some people say we are a clique

   Some people say we are a cul –

   (SUSAN CURTIS *walks through and takes her place in her office.)*

ALL *(spoken, not in rhythm)* Good morning, Miss Curtis.
   (back in rhythm) The year is 1994. The company is Cooney,
   In town they say the secretaries here are a bit loony.

   We are secretaries and we do things secretarial
   And once a month we kill a guy and cut him up for burial
   Sssshhhhh! Sssshhhhh! Sssshhhhh!

   (Lights fade out.)

Scene One
The Office

(A regular workday at the office. The accident sign has been changed to: 1 ACCIDENT-FREE DAY. Throughout the play the numbers increase, culminating in 28. DAWN, PATTY and PEACHES are at their desks. ASHLEY enters.)

DAWN. Hail, Secretary of the Month!

ASHLEY. Oh, cut that would you. October's almost over. Now *you* can claw your way to the top.

DAWN. Me? Never. I can't get Susan Curtis to spit on me. *(She slurps a SlimFast.)* Delicious!

(DAWN, ASHLEY and PEACHES freeze.)

PATTY. *(to audience)* I guess the question I have to ask myself is, "How did a decent girl like me get involved with a cult of murderous secretaries?"

ASHLEY. Patty! *(She laughs and freezes again.)*

PATTY. *(to audience)* I mean, I come from a good family. I have an excellent education most girls would envy, attending one of the finest institutions in the nation with an advanced degree in secretarial sciences with an emphasis on foreign study and international keyboards. That must have been why Susan Curtis hired me. Only the best secretaries in the world work for Coony Lumber Mill in Big Bone, Oregon; the world's largest supplier of fine pine. When I graduated, it was the only place I applied. On a million to one shot, I got lucky.

(SUSAN enters in a hunting hat and a man's plaid hunting jacket, brushes off sawdust and dumps her jacket and hat on ASHLEY's desk. ASHLEY hangs them beside three others. SUSAN goes into her office.)

ASHLEY. What's today?

DAWN. Strawberry.

ASHLEY. Mmmmm.

(DAWN, ASHLEY *and* PEACHES *all click and giggle.*)

PATTY. It's Wednesday.

(They all stop the clicking and giggling. Phone rings.
PATTY *answers.*)

Cooney Lumber Mill. One moment, please. *(over the*
P.A.) Sawmill. Sawmill. Pick up on two.

DAWN. It burns my ass you were hired on as receptionist.
Didn't Mr. Kembunkscher read your resume? I mean,
you only have an advanced degree from one of the
finest schools in the country. You speak six languages,
don't you?

ASHLEY. We all have to start somewhere, Dawn. Right,
Patty?

PATTY. I don't mind, Dawn. Mr. Kembunkscher said he
wanted me to learn the lumber biz from the bottom
up.

DAWN. Bottom up. What do you want to bet those were his
exact words?

(DAWN *and* ASHLEY *click and giggle.*)

PEACHES. Anybody want anything from the watercooler?
I'm going.

ASHLEY. Get me a strawberry from the fridge, will you,
Peaches?

DAWN. And could you put my SlimFast can in the recycling,
please?

PEACHES. Sure, Ashley. Sure, Dawn. *(concentrating hard)*
Strawberry. Recycling. Patty? Anything? I'm going.

PATTY. No, thanks, Peaches.

PEACHES. Suit yourself. Oh, and Patty. A word to the wise.
(She gestures to a giant on-off switch.) This switch controls
the entire mill. Whatever you do, don't turn it off. It
will shut everything down. Take it from me.

(PEACHES *exits.* ASHLEY *and* DAWN *go over to*
PEACHES*'s inbox and sort through her assignments.*)

ASHLEY. Good workout this morning?

DAWN. Jude's class. I missed you.

ASHLEY. Did he kill you?

DAWN. God, my quads and my abs and my whatever you call them, like all over the place. I'm aching.

ASHLEY. He's good, right? I told you.

DAWN. *(handing ASHLEY a document from PEACHES's inbox)* Here, you're better with tables. *(turns to PATTY)*

ASHLEY & DAWN. *(referring to PEACHES)* Charity case.

(ASHLEY and DAWN freeze.)

PATTY. *(to audience)* They all seemed to know each other so well. I thought I'd never fit in. And I wanted to. Almost more than anything. I worried constantly about what they thought of me.

(PEACHES reenters.)

PEACHES. Here you go, Ashley. *(She hands her a strawberry SlimFast.)*

ASHLEY. Thanks, Peaches. Anyone want to split this with me?

PATTY. Is that stuff any good?

ASHLEY. You never tried it?

DAWN. Look at her. Her body's only perfect.

PEACHES. I envy you, Patty. I never see you eating.

PATTY. Oh, I eat plenty. I'm having a salad for lunch today.

DAWN. From where?

PATTY. I made it at home.

PEACHES. Can we see it?

(PATTY shows them the salad.)

Mmmmm. I don't know why I'm so hungry. I'm just getting over my period.

DAWN. That is cool. How do you – ?

PATTY. Salad shooter. It's so easy.

ASHLEY. Don't cucumbers have a lot of calories?

PATTY. I don't know. Probably fifteen calories for a medium cucumber.

ASHLEY. Hmmm. That's what I thought. Still, you manage to stay so thin.

(SUSAN's voice comes over the intercom.)

SUSAN. Ashley, cover the phones. Patty? Join me in my office a moment, will you?

(PATTY goes into SUSAN's office. ASHLEY hits the monitor button on the intercom.)

SUSAN. *(over the intercom)* – 's next Monday sound?

PATTY. *(over the intercom)* That would be fine, Miss Curtis.

SUSAN. *(over the intercom)* Fine, then. That's all for today. You may go.

PATTY. *(over the intercom)* Yes, Miss Curtis. And, thank you.

(ASHLEY quickly turns off the intercom as PATTY enters.)

PATTY. Oh, my god! Oh, my god you won't believe it! They made me a secretary!

ASHLEY. *(through gritted teeth)* Good for you, Patty!

PEACHES. *(hugging her)* Congratulations, Patty!

DAWN. Ashley better watch her back. It won't be long before you're Secretary of the Month. Forget that salad! We're taking you out to the "Sleazy Barn." Our treat! Hats and jackets, girls!

(DAWN, ASHLEY and PEACHES put on their hunting caps and plaid jackets.)

ASHLEY. OW! My hair!

PATTY. Where did you all get those gorgeous jackets?

ASHLEY. It wasn't easy.

DAWN. Yeah, just try getting a lumberjack to part with his jacket!

(DAWN, ASHLEY and PEACHES giggle and click.)

PATTY. Is this some secret secretarial tradition I need to learn about?

DAWN. It's hunting season, Patty.

PEACHES. We don't want to get hit by any bows.

ASHLEY. Actually, Peaches, it's the arrows we're worried about. To the Breezy Barn!

(DAWN, ASHLEY *and* PEACHES *laugh and freeze.*)

PATTY. *(to audience)* That was my first lunch at the Breezy Barn. My first day of being a real true secretary. The very beginning of it all.

(lights out)

Scene Two
The Breezy Barn

(The Breezy Barn, local roadhouse dive. Madonna's "Into the Groove" plays as the girls dance, drink beverage bowls and yell over the music.*)

DAWN. You can have the rest of my beverage bowl, Patty.

PATTY. I don't think I should drink anymore.

ASHLEY. Nonsense! We're celebrating your promotion. Come on! With all you ate, the alcohol won't even affect you!

PEACHES. *(longingly)* She didn't finish her cheeseburger or her potato logs.

PATTY. I offered to share, Peaches. They give you so much food! You all should have had some.

ASHLEY. We do the SlimFast Plan, Patty. It's healthier than food.

PATTY. Why? You're only the most gorgeous secretaries I've ever worked with.

ASHLEY. See? It works.

DAWN. It's what makes us secretaries so strong.

PEACHES. You should try it, Patty.

PATTY. Well, you know, actually, I never needed to lose thirty pounds is the thing. I mean, I was always kind of the shape – since high school I've been this shape. So, I never really need to go on diets.

DAWN. You have a great body, Patty.

PATTY. Thanks, Dawn.

ASHLEY. It's not just for looks, Patty. It's for fitness, too. Do you work out?

PATTY. Not really. I guess I should, huh?

ASHLEY. You ought to get yourself down to the Cooney Recreational Center. They have terrific step classes. Besides, it'll lower the premium on your Cooney Comprehensive Care.

---

*Please see Music Use Note on Page 3.

PATTY. Maybe I'll check it out.

ASHLEY. All right! Drink up, everyone! To Patty!

DAWN & PEACHES. To Patty!

(DAWN *and* PEACHES *hoist their beverage bowls.* DAWN *shares her drink with* PATTY.)

PATTY. This place is wild! I can't believe these drinks!

DAWN. Everything in Big Bone is lumberjack size, Patty. This is a Cooney town and Cooney takes care of the town. You know your performance bonuses start right away. One year of work with no absences and you get to choose one gift from the list: toaster oven?

DAWN, ASHLEY & PEACHES. No!

ASHLEY. A six-month subscription to the *Cooney Chronicle?*

DAWN, ASHLEY & PEACHES. No!

PEACHES. Five shares of Consolidated Cooney Corporation?

DAWN, ASHLEY & PEACHES. No!

DAWN. A Cooney .45 automatic from the firearms collection?

DAWN, ASHLEY & PEACHES. YES!

(ASHLEY *pulls out her giant six-shooter and waves it around as* DAWN *and* PEACHES *whoop and holler.*)

PATTY. I was wondering why you had that pistol in your bag, Ashley.

ASHLEY. I only need eighteen more months of an unblemished attendance record for the assault rifle, fully automatic.

PATTY. You're all so sweet. You make me feel so excited. Like I have nothing to be nervous about.

ASHLEY. There is nothing to be nervous about, except Dawn.

PATTY. Dawn?

ASHLEY. She only goes after secretaries. She wouldn't stoop to a lowly receptionist. Now you're in trouble.

(DAWN, ASHLEY and PEACHES laugh.)

DAWN. Don't listen to her, Patty. Ashley's just jealous because I never asked her out.

PATTY. Dawn! Are you a gay?

DAWN. Does the Big Bone Mall only accept Cooney Cards?

PATTY. I had no idea! You're so pretty.

ASHLEY. She gives the Big Bone Organization for Women a bad name! The lumberjacks think we're ALL lezzies.

PEACHES. You should join BOW, Patty, now that you're gonna be a secretary.

DAWN. You're a Cooney girl, now.

(DAWN, ASHLEY and PEACHES squeal with delight. A secretary whoop.)

PATTY. I'm planning to. Miss Curtis already mentioned it to me.

ASHLEY. *(crushed)* Really? Great.

DAWN. How are you liking Cooney, Patty?

PATTY. This is the best job I've ever had. Miss Curtis is a tough boss, but a really fair one. I never thought I would like working for a woman, but I think Miss Curtis is incredible.

DAWN. Who doesn't?

PEACHES. She's even better, once you get to know her.

ASHLEY. Susan's casual wear is as elegant as her work clothes. She's such a good dresser.

PEACHES. And she smells so good.

PATTY. Yeah, what is that?

ASHLEY. It's "Reckoning" by Don LeBon.

PATTY. Isn't she pretty? She's so pretty.

ASHLEY. I try to be a good dresser, but I'm not so good.

PATTY. Really? I think you look really smart.

ASHLEY. Do you?

PATTY. I do.

ASHLEY. Even in my sweater?

PATTY. Does she really give you cashmere sweaters every time you make Secretary of the Month?

PEACHES. Just the first time.

PATTY. I think it looks really neato. And this blazer –

ASHLEY. Do you like my blazer?

PATTY. You look great. You look really pulled together.

ASHLEY. Good.

PATTY. You look like her.

ASHLEY. *(flattered)* Huh? Do I?

PATTY. Yeah. There's something about you. I don't know. You're just so – both so beautiful.

ASHLEY. Patty. Thanks.

(ASHLEY hugs PATTY and gives her a peck on the cheek.)

PATTY. *(joking)* You're not a gay, too, are you?

(They all laugh.)

DAWN. Come on. Let's dance! Let's do our secretarial duty and drive those lumberjacks wild!

*(Lights out as they all dance to Whitney Houston's "I'm Every Woman."**)*

Scene Three
The Loading Dock

(PATTY *steps out onto the loading dock at the mill. She clutches an invoice in her hand and dings the service bell. She is harassed by the offstage voices of* HANK *and* SANDY.)

HANK. WOOOWEEE.

SANDY. Hey! Hey, you're new around here, aren'tcha?

HANK. We haven't seen you before. You're a very attractive lady. Do you know that?

SANDY. Hey, I think my friend here likes you.

HANK. You look nice in that dress. I'll tell you that much.

SANDY. How 'bout a pretty smile for us guys working over here.

HANK. Yeah. Come on, honey. How 'bout a little smile.

SANDY. Come on. One smile ain't gonna hurtcha.

HANK. Loosen up, for Chrissakes. All we're asking for is a smile. What's your fuckin' problem?

SANDY. Hey sweetheart, do I have to come out there and make you smile?

PATTY. Fuck you!

HANK. Oooooh.

SANDY. You're a tough one.

(PATTY *turns to leave and runs headlong into* BUZZ BENIKEE.)

PATTY. Oh!

BUZZ. Geez! Sorry! Are you...

PATTY. Let me go...

BUZZ. Is that an invoice? Who sent you...?

SANDY. Hey, Buzz! Get her number, man. Get her phone number.

HANK. Yeah! Find out who she is.

BUZZ. *(to the men, in a deep voice of authority)* Hey! Cut that out, you guys.

SANDY. Oh, come on, man. She's a total fox.

HANK. Get her phone number. Find out who she is.

BUZZ. I'm serious, you animals, cut it! I mean now!

HANK & SANDY. *(muttering)* Yeah. All right. Whatever.

PATTY. What's wrong with those people?

BUZZ. Here, let me take that. *(He takes the invoice.)* My personal apologies, ma'am. Who the hell sent you out here on the loading dock all by yourself?

PATTY. No one sent me. I just thought I'd take care of this myself. I'm new at Cooney. I just made secretary.

BUZZ. We're up in the woods a lot of the time – we don't see too many women. I know that's no excuse but the company hires a lot of the guys from the prison or halfway houses in town. They're good loggers but they don't have the best manners, I guess.

PATTY. I'll say.

BUZZ. I'm Buzz Benikee.

PATTY. I'm Patty. Patty Johnson. What's a nice guy like you doing in a place like this?

BUZZ. I grew up in Big Bone. Mr. Cooney was like a second father to me and offered me the job as foreman when I got back from the Peace Corps. There's not a lot of intellectual stimulation but I do love being outdoors.

PATTY. Well, it's nice to meet you, Buzz.

(She shakes his hand.)

You seem like a really terrific guy.

BUZZ. And you have really soft skin.

PATTY. Thanks.

BUZZ. Oh, oh, Jesus. I can't believe – you know, I just took a sexual harassment workshop and that's exactly the kind of thing I'm *not* supposed to say!

PATTY. No, no, no, no, no. I'm flattered. I mean, I'm no feminist. I can take a compliment.

BUZZ. You're terrific, you know that? What's a nice secretary like you doing in a place like this?

(They both laugh.)

PATTY. Thanks, Buzz.

BUZZ. You wouldn't...I mean, I hope this isn't out of line but would you...oh, hell, I'll just say it. Would you like to go to the movies with me tomorrow, Patty Johnson? There's a little art cinema in town. I think that Dutch film, *The Nasty Girl,* is showing there now.

PATTY. Oh, *ik wil graag naar de film met je,* Buzz.

BUZZ. What?

PATTY. It's Dutch for. "I'd love to."

BUZZ. You are something! Patty Johnson. Pretty, pretty Patty Johnson. Until tomorrow.

PATTY. Until tomorrow.

(lights out)

Scene Four
Back in the Office

(The next day. The sign on the wall now reads: ...3 ACCIDENT-FREE DAYS. DAWN, PATTY *and* ASHLEY *are working.* PEACHES *enters balancing four cups.)*

PEACHES. Somebody help me. Somebody help me. Somebody help me. Oh. Oh. Oh. Shit.

*(*DAWN *takes one of the cups.)*

Oh, good. Thanks. Oh, OK. Whew, that was a close one. Did everybody get what they wanted?

ASHLEY. Did you put the Equals in here?

PEACHES. Oh, yeah. *(She spills her drink on her desk.)* Oops. Oh, not my picture of Dusty! Oh shit! It's ruined! His wife will never give me another one.

PATTY. His wife...?

PEACHES. Oh, his wife, his ex-wife, his widow, whatever...

PATTY. He's dead?

ASHLEY. *(pointedly changing the subject)* So what did you do this weekend, Dawn?

PEACHES. Yeah, Patty. He's been dead about three days now... *(She gestures to the "accident calendar.")*

DAWN. Uh, Cooney Rec. Bonita's class.

ASHLEY. Which one?

DAWN. Buns and boobs. What did you do this weekend, Patty?

PATTY. Huh? I'm sorry. What? I'm sorry. How did he die, Peaches?

ASHLEY. Accident, of course. Oh, we lose a lot of men that way. Almost everyone here has lost someone to the heavy machinery.

DAWN. Yeah, they never found his body. They think it was dragged off by a big cat. *(handing* PATTY *a stack of papers)* Patty, can you take half of this?

PATTY. Sure, Dawn.

(SUSAN enters. The secretaries snap into work mode.)

SUSAN. *(referring to* PATTY*'s typing)* Slow down, Patty. This is only the beginning. How fast do you type again?

PATTY. A hundred and twelve words a minute.

ASHLEY. *(begrudgingly)* Not bad.

SUSAN. Incredible! Would you mind…Can I look at your hands for a minute? Exquisite. These wrists. No carpal tunnel?

*(*PATTY *shakes her head.)*

Never? Amazing. These tendons in your forearms…

PATTY. Heredity. Guess I was just cut out to be a secretary.

SUSAN. *(feeling up* PATTY*'s arms to her neck)* Strong shoulders, too. No neck strain. You must have excellent posture.

PATTY. That's nothing. We learned that first year.

SUSAN. Of course. *(noticing* PATTY*'s undergarment)* Is this Victoria's Secret?

PATTY. *(blushing)* Yes. I noticed you had a lot of their catalogs in your office.

ASHLEY. I love Victoria's Secret. Don't you, Peaches?

SUSAN. I do order a lot. Do you like the way I dress?

PATTY. Yes! I guess. I mean –

SUSAN. It's OK. I love compliments. You should learn to accept compliments, Patty. I bet you get a lot of them. This is beautiful on you. Isn't it, girls? Let me know the number. Maybe I'll order one. What's it made of?

*(*SUSAN *puts her hand down the front of* PATTY*'s dress.)*

Mmmmm. Nice. Comfortable?

PATTY. *(entranced)* Mmmmm. I really love you, Miss Curtis.

SUSAN. *(feigning embarrassment)* Oh my.

PATTY. *(also embarrassed)* No, I mean. I admire you. I admire you and your work and your – the way you are. I wish – I wish I was more like you.

SUSAN. Thank you, Patty. See? That's how easy it is to accept a compliment. Want to practice?

PATTY. *(laughs)* Oh, well. I don't think –

SUSAN. Nonsense. Ready? Patty, you have wonderful taste in clothes.

PATTY. Really?

SUSAN. No, Patty. You say, "Thank you." Accept the compliment, don't question it. Patty, your typing skills are superb.

PATTY. Oh. I – thank you. Thank you very much.

SUSAN. Good. Patty, your breasts are better than any set of implants.

PATTY. Miss Curtis!

SUSAN. Just say, "Thank you."

PATTY. Thank you.

SUSAN. Better. But I can see I'm going to have to work on you. I'm getting a little light-headed.

(turns PATTY*'s hand and looks at her watch)*

Well, no wonder, it's way past my lunchtime. Would you like to join me for a shake in the cafeteria?

PATTY. Can you believe? I've never tried it.

SUSAN. No, well, with a figure like yours I don't know why you would have.

*(*PATTY *blushes.)*

PATTY. Well, I could say the same about you.

SUSAN. I drink them because they're fast, easy and delicious! And they're better than food, really. They were invented by a doctor.

ASHLEY. Susan? What about the Cooney Cares Foundation luncheon?

SUSAN. Oh! Right. I'll tell you, Patty, if my head wasn't bolted on...Well, let's take a rain check on that lunch, sound good? Don't let me forget that, all right, Ashley?

ASHLEY. I'll make a note.

SUSAN. In the meantime, here's my Cooney Gold Card. *(She hands it to* ASHLEY.*)* Why don't you girls fix Patty up with a shake and show her around the Big Bone Mall? Get Patty something special. Get yourselves something special.

ASHLEY. Susan, we couldn't.

DAWN. *(snatching the card)* Yes, we could.

PEACHES. Thanks, Susan.

SUSAN. Toodles.

(All freeze except **PATTY.***)*

PATTY. *(to audience)* I got my first taste of Big Bone on Susan Curtis's Gold Card. I could see why she'd appeared on the cover of Executive Secretary Quarterly three times. She really knew how to motivate. I had a lot to learn.

(lights out)

Scene Five
The Video Store

(PATTY is in the video store. SUSAN enters wearing her hunting hat and plaid jacket.)

SUSAN. Patty? How nice to see you. Imagine running into you in the Dutch filmmakers' section. What are you renting?

PATTY. Oh, I don't know. I haven't decided yet. Maybe this.

SUSAN. *A Question of Silence?* Hmmm. Sounds intense.

PATTY. I guess. Last night I went to see *The Nasty Girl.*

SUSAN. Now, that sounds like my kind of movie.

(They laugh.)

Oh well, a video on a Saturday night. A couple of lonely single girls, aren't we?

PATTY. Oh, I'm not lonely, Miss Curtis. I often watch a video by myself on a Saturday night.

SUSAN. Now, Patty, do you mean to tell me you wouldn't rather be cuddling up with a big strong lumberjack on the sofa watching *The Bodyguard?*

PATTY. Well, that does sound nice, now that you mention it.

SUSAN. Of course it does, Patty. You don't have to hide your feelings from me. I know why you're at the mill. For the same reason I came to the mill. My mother was a secretary, my sister was a secretary. It's a good way to meet lumberjacks.

(They laugh together.)

Now listen. The idea of going home and watching *Blood Sport* all by myself and stuffing myself with popcorn is about as appealing as having my pubic hair plucked. But it'd sure be a lot more fun if you'd come home and watch with me.

PATTY. Miss Curtis, I don't want to impose.

SUSAN. Call me Susan, Patty. We're not in the office anymore.

PATTY. Very well, Susan. I think I will take you up on that offer.

(SUSAN *puts her arm in* PATTY*'s. She puts her hat on* PATTY*'s head.*)

SUSAN. We're gonna have to get you a jacket. It's dangerous out there.

(*They exit. Blackout.*)

Scene Six
The Chorus

DAWN, ASHLEY & PEACHES. *(at their desks, rhythmically typing and chanting)*
Susan says, "Reveal, Patty." Alt F3.
Patty Flushes, Right. Alt F6.
Bold F6, Move F4, Susan. Watch out, Patty

Shift F1, Set Up.

(blackout)

Scene Seven
First Club Meeting

(The office, after work hours. The sign now reads: 5 ACCIDENT-FREE DAYS. DAWN, ASHLEY and PEACHES are wearing pink sweaters. They are milling, clicking and giggling. PATTY enters. She's also wearing a pink sweater.)

ASHLEY. Forget something, Patty?

PATTY. Isn't this the meeting of the Big Bone Organization for Women?

PEACHES. Patty! You got your sweater.

DAWN. Congratulations, Patty.

ASHLEY. *(disingenuous)* Patty Johnson, Secretary of the Month. That's terrific. Congratulations, Patty.

PEACHES. I'm so happy for you. You look so beautiful. Secretary of the Month. I haven't been Secretary of the Month since before they invented the carriage return. I've got a little bit of an appearance issue. It doesn't matter. Doesn't she look great, Dawn?

DAWN. *(staring at PATTY)* What? Oh, yeah.

PATTY. I'm so embarrassed. Secretary of the Month and I've only been here a week. Ashley, I don't know what to say. You were Secretary of the Month for such a long time, I understand.

ASHLEY. Yes, well, that's the way it goes. I'm sure you've done plenty to earn it.

(They all sit, except PATTY.)

DAWN. Here, Patty. You can sit by me.

(PATTY sits next to DAWN.)

PATTY. I'm a little nervous. I've never joined a group of only women before, unless you count the Brownies.

DAWN. Oh, Brownies count.

PEACHES. Wanna shake, Patty?

PATTY. No, thanks. I just had dinner.

PEACHES. Dinner?

PATTY. Yeah, you know, the sensible dinner part of the plan. *(She looks at* **DAWN***'s SlimFast can.)*

DAWN. I would kill for a square meal right now.

PATTY. You can't read this one; it's all scratched up.

ASHLEY. That happens during shipping. Anyway, who needs it. We find the shakes are enough.

PATTY. You mean all you eat are the shakes?

PEACHES. Sometimes we eat the bars too. They're a terrific binder.

*(***SUSAN*** enters. ***ASHLEY*** jumps up and takes ***SUSAN***'s hunting coat and hat and hangs them up.)*

SUSAN. Evening, ladies.

DAWN, ASHLEY, PEACHES & PATTY. Good evening, Susan.

SUSAN. Sorry to be tardy. My budget meeting went a little late. Welcome to your first BOW meeting, Patty. That sweater looks terrific on you. Oh my! What a darling pin!

PATTY. Oh, it's nothing. I made it. It's something my mother taught me. See, it's just a walnut with these little googly eyes…Would you like it?

SUSAN. Oh, Patty, I couldn't.

PATTY. No, seriously. Here.

*(***PATTY*** puts the pin on ***SUSAN***.)*

I've got about a million of them at home.

SUSAN. Thanks, Patty. And thank your mother!

*(***SUSAN*** and ***PATTY*** laugh.)*

I trust everyone congratulated Patty today.

*(All except ***PATTY*** applaud.)*

DAWN. Hail, Secretary of the Month.

PATTY. Oh, Dawn, please. Now I know how Ashley felt all those months.

ASHLEY. Oh, pressure, pressure, pressure.

PEACHES. You're doing great, Patty.

PATTY. Thanks, Peaches.

SUSAN. Well, shall we begin?

(They all take hands and bow their heads for the invocation.)

We thank you for the opportunity to meet for shakes and fellowship. Please help us to word process without error, to follow the SlimFast plan, and to make it through that time of the month together.

(The invocation is over and they release hands.)

And speaking of that time of the month, since we're just completing our last cycle, no bloodstains anyone, I hope.

*(All except **PATTY** click and giggle.)*

PATTY. Wait a minute, you mean you're all on the same cycle?

SUSAN. I'm sure you'll sync up soon, Patty. It's what happens when we women spend so much of our time together.

PATTY. I have heard that. I guess I never spent that much time with my women friends before.

PEACHES. *(to **SUSAN**)* I have a problem with bloodstains.

(There is a tense pause.)

PATTY. Well, Peaches, just rinse them right away with a little cold water, and never, under any circumstances, never EVER rinse them with hot. That sets the stain.

PEACHES. Thanks, Patty.

SUSAN. Isn't she terrific? Let's get down to business. Ashley?

ASHLEY. OK, on tonight's agenda we have ergonomic chairs committee, international relations, blood drive, tampon collection, and clean up and disposal from our monthly…event.

SUSAN. Fine, Ashley. Let's begin by taking up the collection.

(As the girls reach under their skirts, remove their bloody tampons and deposit them in a Ziploc bag provided by ASHLEY.*)*

Patty, you studied Japanese all four years, isn't that right?

PATTY. *(horrified)* Uh, yeah.

SUSAN. Ron Kembunkscher and I were arguing. Is it "*mosu-KAI*" or "*moSUkai*"?

PATTY. Um, what?

SUSAN. Oh, my accent is so terrible you probably can't even understand what I'm saying.

*(*ASHLEY *gives* SUSAN *the bag of tampons, which she puts in her briefcase.)*

Ashley. Thank you. Next item. Dawn. Ergonomic chairs?

DAWN. Right. Idaho.

SUSAN. You checked with –

DAWN. Yup. Nope.

SUSAN. OK. I'll go with that. Good work, Dawn. International relations. Peaches?

PEACHES. We blamed it on customs.

SUSAN. And there's no –

PEACHES. There is. But they can't trace it back to them.

SUSAN. Terrific. Anything else?

ASHLEY. Just a reminder that the blood drive is underway in the cafeteria every afternoon. Team BOW was number one last year, we can do it again.

*(*DAWN, ASHLEY *and* PEACHES *whoop.)*

SUSAN. Remember, ladies, there's cookies and juice down there. So be careful. All right, let's get Patty assigned to a committee. Anything sound interesting, Patty?

DAWN. You can be on ergonomic chairs with me, Patty.

PATTY. Thanks, Dawn. Maybe I will. What about monthly event? I think I might have an idea for that.

SUSAN. I'm sure we'd all love to hear it.

(All except PATTY *giggle and click.)*

Go ahead, Patty.

PATTY. Well, I feel a little awkward. I guess it's because I'm new and everything. But I was thinking about a health and beauty night. I used to organize them in school.

*(*PEACHES, ASHLEY *and* DAWN *look to* SUSAN.*)*

SUSAN. I think that sounds like just the kind of thing this group needs to bring us all closer together.

PEACHES. Good idea, Patty.

SUSAN. I propose a health and beauty night with Patty in charge. All those in favor?

DAWN, ASHLEY, PEACHES & SUSAN. Aye.

SUSAN. Good. I can't wait to see what you have in store for us. Well, ladies, until next week.

DAWN, ASHLEY, PEACHES & SUSAN. Shakes are blessedly allowed.

(All sip.)

Delicious.

(All stand and clap.)

ASHLEY. Good meeting, Susan.

PATTY. Dawn, are you doing anything later tonight?

DAWN. No. Why?

PATTY. I was wondering if you could drop me at the CooneyPlex 12. I'm meeting Buzz there later.

DAWN. *(disappointed)* Oh. Sure.

SUSAN. Oh, I don't know where my head is. Patty, I almost forgot to give you this.

(She hands PATTY *a package.)*

It's your BOW beginners kit. It has your "Welcome to BOW" video, your organ donor card, guidelines for dress code and nail length –

PATTY. *(reaching into the bag)* OW! I pricked myself.

PEACHES. Oh, it's your button, Patty.

PATTY. *(reading the button)* "Hugs not intercourse"?

SUSAN. It goes with this.

> (SUSAN *presents* PATTY *with a piece of paper from the kit.*)

> We just need your signature right here.

DAWN. It's a celibacy agreement, Patty.

PATTY. I don't understand.

SUSAN. One thing we appreciate in BOW is healthy relationships. We all date, of course. But a girl needs to know how to say no and the rule just makes it easier.

ASHLEY. You want to keep your sweater, don't you, Patty?

DAWN. Here's a pen, Patty.

> (PATTY *signs the agreement. Lights out.*)

Scene Eight
Patty and Buzz at the Loading Dock

(The loading dock. Stifled sex sounds are heard from behind a wall of lumber. PATTY and BUZZ emerge, post-coital, PATTY's hose are around her ankles.)

BUZZ. Patty, you're incredible. I don't know what got into you. I've never met anyone like you. *(holds up a used condom)* Look, Patty, this could be our son.

PATTY. Buzz.

BUZZ. I know, I'm a nut.

PATTY. You're a walnut.

BUZZ. You're a peanut!

PATTY. You're a cashew!

BUZZ. You're a Jordan Almond!

PATTY. Ooo! My favorite! You're an M&M chocolate-covered peanut!

BUZZ. A green one!

PATTY. *(looking at her watch)* I've got to get back. Ashley gives me a look if I'm more than five minutes late.

BUZZ. How are you getting along with those girls?

PATTY. Oh, great. I just joined their service organization, BOW. They have some odd little customs but mostly it's really great.

BUZZ. Some of those secretaries can be pretty nasty. They've gone through a lot of new girls over the years.

PATTY. Hmm. They've been really nice to me.

BUZZ. Well, just watch yourself.

(The sound of an alarm bell.)

Oh. Gotta get back to pulping. 'Bye.

(They kiss. They keep kissing and saying good-bye until they finally tear themselves away. The lumber wall is pushed back to reveal ASHLEY, spying. Lights out.)

Scene Nine
Patty and Peaches in the Bathroom

(**PEACHES** *is in the stall of the office ladies' room.* **PATTY** *enters.*)

PEACHES. Damn him. Damn him. Damn him.

PATTY. Peaches, what's wrong? Are you all right?

PEACHES. Damn him to hell.

PATTY. What happened, Peaches? Can I help you?

PEACHES. No, Patty. Not unless you're Susan Curtis you can't help me. (*She comes out of the stall.*)

PATTY. Did you…did Mr. Kembunkscher say something?

PEACHES. Maybe. Maybe he did. Susan said he did. She said Mr. Kembunkscher isn't happy with me. He isn't happy with my performance.

PATTY. Oh.

PEACHES. She said he said I'm not the right size. Can you believe that, Patty? Mr. Kembunkscher. Fat, old, baldy-top Mr. Kembunkscher can tell me I'm not the right size. I can't be over a size twelve. Susan said he said none of the girls can be over a twelve. Damn him. I bet that fat old hog hasn't ever even tried to diet. I bet he's eaten three meals a day for his whole goddamn life with snacks in between. Fat hog. Fat hog. I'd like to prick him with a needle.

PATTY. Peaches…I think you're fine the way you are. We all come in different shapes and sizes. Mr. Kembunkscher has no right to dictate what size his employees should be. Really. It's not legal.

PEACHES. Sure. Maybe in a court of law. But in Big Bone there's only one law. Cooney law. And we better obey or else there's hell to pay.

PATTY. I'm sure Susan doesn't see it that way.

PEACHES. No. Susan is on my side. She said so. She said, "There's no way I'm going to let Kembunkscher get away with this." She said that.

PATTY. Good. See then? There's nothing to worry about. Susan can stand up to Mr. Kembunkscher.

PEACHES. She said that for now I should try to slim down. Patty, I have to stop eating solids. I can't help myself. I crave them. I get sick off the shakes. Susan said you could help me.

PATTY. I don't know, Peaches. I don't think it's a good idea to drink the shakes only.

PEACHES. But help me anyway, all right, Patty? If you see me with a bear claw or a bag of mixed nuts in my hands, just give me a little slap on my face, OK? Just a little slap so I'll associate it with eating solids, OK?

PATTY. Peaches, I'm not going to slap you.

PEACHES. Oh, come on. I'd ask Dawn but she's real busy right now with the invoices. And Susan says she's done it long enough and it's time for one of the other girls to do it. Oh, come on, Patty. Please. I don't know what I'll do if I lose this job.

PATTY. This is insane. I won't hit you, Peaches.

PEACHES. OK. Just till I get down to a ten. That won't take long. Five days of no solids and I'm sure I'll lose thirty. Please? Won't you? Patty, if I lose this job I don't know what I'll do. I'll – I'll kill myself, Patty, I swear. That's how I feel. I'll put myself on the saw board like that other secretary. I will. I'll do it.

PATTY. All right. All right, Peaches. I'll help you.

PEACHES. Oh, god, you will? Oh god. Thank you, Patty. Thank you. Will you slap me?

PATTY. Yes.

PEACHES. You will?

PATTY. Yes.

PEACHES. Can we try it now?

(**PATTY** *stares, incredulous.*)

For practice.

(**PATTY** *gives* **PEACHES** *a tap on the cheek.*)

PEACHES. *(cont.)* See. That's why I had you try it. That's not hard enough and it won't work.

(PATTY gives PEACHES a stronger tap.)

Patty!

(PEACHES slaps PATTY hard. PATTY slaps PEACHES back even harder.)

There. Yes. That was good. Thank you, Patty. Thank you.

(lights out)

Scene Ten
HHH Health and Beauty Night

(SUSAN, ASHLEY, DAWN, PEACHES *and* PATTY *are at the Hollyhock Hideaway Hotel dressed in Victoria's Secret lingerie.* SUSAN *is on the bed with a spinner for the game Twister. The others are in a tangle on the floor.*)

SUSAN. Right foot, yellow.

PEACHES. No way! I can't.

ASHLEY. Dawn! I was gonna go there.

DAWN. Too slow.

(DAWN, ASHLEY, PEACHES *and* PATTY *collapse, laughing really hard.*)

ASHLEY. We better keep it down. The hotel manager is gonna think we're having an orgy in here.

DAWN. Don't I wish.

PATTY. Dawn!

DAWN. A girl can dream, can't she?

PEACHES. *(jumping on the bed)* Magic fingers! Now let's do magic fingers!

DAWN. If we turn on the magic fingers, I think I might be sick. I ate too much Jenny Craig popcorn.

PATTY. Me too, Dawn. I feel like a giant human popcorn.

DAWN. Me too. I feel exactly the same.

PATTY. That's just how I feel.

ASHLEY. I don't see what playing Twister has to do with health and beauty, Patty.

PATTY. I think it helps to break the ice. Ashley, I don't think I've ever seen you laugh so hard.

(She tickles ASHLEY.*)*

PEACHES. *(indicating her lingerie)* Susan provided the beauty part. Thanks, Susan.

SUSAN. I hope I got the sizes right.

ASHLEY. Mine's perfect.

PATTY. *(lifting two cucumbers)* Here's the health part!

DAWN. Mmmm. I could make a joke, but I won't.

PEACHES. Dawn!

DAWN. What? I think that's healthy.

PATTY. Cucumber is really good for your skin. It's very cleansing.

SUSAN. I like an avocado facial. My dry skin loves the moisture of the avocado.

PATTY. *(picking up a horrendously bloodstained towel)* Whose towel is this?

PEACHES. What? Oh, it's mine.

PATTY. Are these bloodstains all over it?

PEACHES. Oh, yeah. That was – um, from before you told me about the cold water.

(ASHLEY grabs the towel and gives it to SUSAN, who hides it. PEACHES starts to laugh hysterically.)

DAWN. Have another Zima, Peaches.

PEACHES. I know! Let's play Truth or Dare. Should we? Remember Truth or Dare, anyone?

ASHLEY. That was not my favorite game.

SUSAN. I don't think I'm familiar with that. How do you play?

PEACHES. Oh, it's easy. Someone asks you a question and – how do you play again?

DAWN. Someone asks you a personal question and then you have to decide if you're going to tell the truth or take a dare. It was always a staple at slumber parties.

SUSAN. That does sound fun.

PATTY. OK, I've got one. Ashley.

ASHLEY. I don't like it really.

SUSAN. All right, then. We won't ask you anything, Ashley. How about you, Dawn?

ASHLEY. No! Ask me a question.

PATTY. OK. How many boyfriends have you had?

ASHLEY. Oh god, Patty. Truth. That one's easy.

PEACHES. Ashley holds the record.

DAWN. Go ahead. Show her, Ashley.

(ASHLEY *unfurls a three-foot-long snapshot holder chock full of lumberjacks.*)

PEACHES. Oh, look, Chip and Woody…

PATTY. Wow! It must be hard running into all those ex-boyfriends.

ASHLEY. Oh, it's not a problem really.

(*All except* PATTY *giggle and click.*)

SUSAN. Ashley's an expert at detachment.

DAWN. Come on, Patty. You can come up with a better one than that.

PATTY. OK. You.

DAWN. Me?

PATTY. You.

DAWN. I'll take the dare.

PEACHES. But you don't even know the question.

DAWN. I don't have to know the question. I always take the dare.

PATTY. OK. I dare you to tell the truth.

DAWN. *(laughing)* What truth?

PATTY. OK. If you could sleep with anyone in BOW, including Susan, who would it be?

PEACHES. Oooohh. I know it's not me. Is it Patty, Dawn?

PATTY. Peaches, come on. Let Dawn answer.

PEACHES. It is. It is Patty. Look at her.

DAWN. No way!

PEACHES. She's blushing.

DAWN. Cut it out! I don't think about Patty in that way. I mean, I feel really close to her and so it would be like doing it with my sister or something.

ASHLEY. Maybe you should take your sister to Choices with you, Dawn.

PATTY. What's Choices?

ASHLEY. It's a bar. In Beaver Lick.

PEACHES. Beaver Lick! That's a long way to go, just to go to a bar.

DAWN. All right! Next victim.

ASHLEY. New girl! New girl!

PEACHES. Huddle.

(DAWN, ASHLEY and PEACHES huddle.)

DAWN. OK. We've got it. Patty Johnson, truth or dare.

PATTY. Truth.

DAWN. OK. When was the last time you had sex?

PATTY. Oh, god. Dare. I'll take the dare.

ASHLEY. No. Patty. Too late. You picked truth.

SUSAN. Come on, Patty. Play the game.

DAWN, ASHLEY & PEACHES. Yeah, truth! Truth! Truth!

PATTY. It was in senior year. In secretarial school.

DAWN, ASHLEY & PEACHES. Yeaaaah?…

PATTY. This guy – Mike – we went out for about a month.

ASHLEY & PEACHES. Yeaah?

DAWN. We want the gory details.

ASHLEY. Size of member!

PEACHES. Did you blow him, Patty?

PATTY. I don't know. It was medium. We just fooled around. Look, I don't want to talk about this anymore.

ASHLEY. Oooh. Touched a nerve.

PATTY. Some things are private.

ASHLEY. Not in BOW, Patty.

SUSAN. That's enough, Ashley. Patty answered our question. She told the truth, like we asked.

(awkward pause)

PEACHES. I guess no one wants to play anymore.

PATTY. No! I get to ask one back, right? That's how it works, right?

DAWN. Sure, Patty.

PATTY. OK, Susan. Truth.

SUSAN. I find it's always easier to tell the truth.

PATTY. OK. Why do you collect our tampons?

(tense pause)

SUSAN. It's research. I'm writing a book about female office workers. I have a management theory based on using people's natural body rhythms to facilitate a more cohesive work unit in the office.

PATTY. Really?

PEACHES. Really?

SUSAN. You asked for the truth, Patty.

ASHLEY. I'm typing the manuscript. She's almost finished.

PATTY. That's incredible.

SUSAN. Isn't it?

PEACHES. Hey, look everybody! It's Patrick Swayze!

(They all rush to the TV. Lights out.)

Scene Eleven
The Chorus

(In the office. After hours. PATTY *searches with a flashlight.)*

PATTY. Search Dusty
Access Denied
Search Dusty
Override
Search Woody
Search Chip

(She opens a drawer and discovers a chain saw.)

Widow/Orphan Protection
Off.

(blackout)

Scene Twelve
Back in the Office

(**ASHLEY** *is sitting at her desk. The accident sign now reads: 16 ACCIDENT-FREE DAYS. It is late, and* **ASHLEY** *is working on a little statue of* **SUSAN** *made out of office supplies.* **SUSAN** *is in her office getting ready to leave.*)

ASHLEY. *(talking to herself)* Just a minute. Just a minute. Susan, don't leave yet. I'm almost finished. I need a head. It's easy for Patty to make things; she had a mother. (**ASHLEY** *finds a binder clip and uses it for the statue's head.*) There. Oh, not bad. *(imagining that she's presenting the doll to Susan)* Here you are, Susan. Oh, it's just a little something I…Beautiful? Susan, I think you're exaggerating. I mean it's no googly-eye pin or anything. I think we ought to give Patty an "A" for effort. An "F" for faker? You think you know someone and it turns out they aren't sweet and nice after all. Just rotten and bad like everyone else. Still, you shouldn't compare me and Patty like that. It's not fair. It's not fair. Patty doesn't know you like I do. I know you. Don't forget how well I know you. I know all about you, Susan.

SUSAN. *(entering from her office)* Ashley, how's the Annual Report? I want the first draft on my desk by 9.00 a.m. sharp.

ASHLEY. I've finished it already, Susan. I was just about to come in and deliver it.

SUSAN. Well?

ASHLEY. Oh, well, actually, the reason I hadn't given it to you yet is that, well, I've been working on another project for you.

SUSAN. Yes?

ASHLEY. It's a creative project.

(**ASHLEY** *shoves the statue into* **SUSAN**'s *hands.* **SUSAN** *stares at it, perplexed.*)

I call her "Woman of Steel." It's you.

SUSAN. What can I say, Ashley? It's really something.

ASHLEY. You can have it. I've got a million of them at home.

SUSAN. Thank you.

ASHLEY. It expresses how I feel about you. The respect I feel.

SUSAN. Thank you, Ashley.

ASHLEY. I know you like your desk to be clear but I was thinking a good place for it would be next to your nameplate. And, if you want, you can use the briefcase as a paper-clip dispenser. It's set up for that.

SUSAN. Ashley, you know I count on you. Especially now. It's a very delicate time.

ASHLEY. Oh, I know, I know.

SUSAN. When was the last time we updated your files?

ASHLEY. Six weeks ago yesterday.

SUSAN. Six weeks? Really.

ASHLEY. Yes, Susan. *(She starts unbuttoning her own blouse.)*

SUSAN. How could I have let it slip by for such a long time? Let's see. We'll need an upper and a lower if it's been six weeks. And don't wiggle around. It comes out blurred. And make sure you wipe the glass with Windex when you're through.

ASHLEY. Yes, Susan. An upper and a lower? *(She stands there with her blouse open.)*

SUSAN. That's what I said.

ASHLEY. Enlarged?

SUSAN. The usual one-hundred percent will be fine, Ashley.

(ASHLEY exits. We hear the sound of a copier, and a flashing bright light is seen offstage. ASHLEY enters and hands some photocopies to SUSAN.)

SUSAN. Um-hmm. Look at these. Pectorals with nipples.

ASHLEY. Thank you, Susan.

SUSAN. Why don't you knock off tonight? We'll make Patty do the second draft in the morning.

ASHLEY. *(putting her coat on, pleased)* Oh, but Susan, it will take her all day.

SUSAN. She can skip lunch then. I want to see you at Cooney Rec tomorrow, keeping up the good work.

ASHLEY. You're the boss. Good night, Susan.

(SUSAN makes the statue wave.)

SUSAN. Good night.

(ASHLEY exits. SUSAN drops the statue into the garbage. Lights out.)

Scene Thirteen
Patty and Buzz on the Phone

(The office. The accident sign reads: 27 ACCIDENT-
FREE DAYS. ASHLEY is working. PEACHES is sneaking
a little food. The phone rings. PEACHES answers it with
her mouth full of food.)

PEACHES. Cooney Lumber Mill. Just a moment, please.
Patty! Phone!

(PATTY sees PEACHES eating and without hesitating
slaps her hard. PEACHES hands PATTY the phone.)

Thank you.

(BUZZ walks onstage holding a phone.)

BUZZ. Hi, Patty.

PATTY. Oh, hi. Hi, how are you?

BUZZ. I'm great. What are you doing?

PATTY. I'm working, silly.

BUZZ. Me too. Only I couldn't stop thinking about you.
You were great today, Patty.

PATTY. Oh, thanks, thanks a lot. You too.

BUZZ. What did you like best, Patty?

PATTY. Well, I really can't say.

BUZZ. I know it's hard to pick one moment. It was all so
perfect.

PATTY. Look, you probably shouldn't call here.

BUZZ. Is Curtis on your tail?

PATTY. No. It's just – I have work to do, is all.

BUZZ. Christ, Patty, it's just a job.

PATTY. No, it's not. It's more than a job. But you wouldn't
understand that –

BUZZ. Easy, easy. What is with you, anyway?

PATTY. I'm sorry. I'm sorry I'm such a bitch. There's so
much going on here. Where are you guys today?

BUZZ. We're about six miles north of Forky Knoll. We're
pretty cold up here today.

PATTY. Listen, have you ever been in an accident? On the job, I mean.

BUZZ. Knock wood, I haven't. We've lost a lot of guys over the years. I mean a lot. It seems we can't make twenty-nine days without something horrible happening. Why do you ask?

PATTY. I'd just hate for anything to happen to you.

BUZZ. Hey, hey – don't worry about me. I know how to take care of myself. Besides, I'm mostly in that little mobile office.

PATTY. I gotta go. I'll see you tomorrow, OK? And – be careful, Buzz.

BUZZ. I promise I won't go out without my slicker.

(**PATTY** and **BUZZ** hang up. **BUZZ** exits.)

ASHLEY. Who was that, Patty?

PATTY. Buzz.

ASHLEY. You two are going pretty steady now, aren't you?

PATTY. I wouldn't say that, Ashley. We're really just friends.

ASHLEY. Friends – in that nineties kind of way.

PATTY. Now what is that supposed to mean?

ASHLEY. I read about it in *Self,* Patty. In the nineties, men and women can sleep with each other and just be friends.

PATTY. We're not sleeping together.

ASHLEY. Right. You're not sleeping together.

PEACHES. No, there's no time to sleep on your lunch hour. They just do it and come back to work.

ASHLEY. I'd be careful if I were you, Patty. Susan is pretty strict about certain rules.

PATTY. This rule is stupid. I mean, it's not fair. It's easier when no one's asking you out.

ASHLEY. Are you saying we're ugly?

PATTY. You're twisting everything. It's just that I don't see why I should have to answer to the club. It's not like I'm the only one around here with needs.

(**PEACHES** *and* **ASHLEY** *giggle and click to each other, then they freeze.*)

PATTY. *(cont.)* *(to audience)* You know, sometimes I look at Buzz in his work boots and jacket and I think he looks attractive. Then I stop and I question myself: is it Buzz I'm attracted to, or his jacket?

(**PEACHES** *and* **ASHLEY** *unfreeze and resume giggling and clicking.*)

Sometimes you girls really give me the creeps. I'm taking fifteen.

(**PATTY** *gets up and starts to exit the office. She bumps into* **DAWN**.)

DAWN. Whoa! You OK, Patty? What's wrong?

PATTY. Dawn. You know, sometimes I feel like one of the group and sometimes I feel like some kind of a freak or something.

DAWN. Let me guess. Ashlickey?

PATTY. Uh-huh.

DAWN. Well, wait until you've been around longer. Then you'll really feel like a freak.

(She starts to rub **PATTY***'s shoulders.)*

Wow, you're tight as a drum. You can't let her get under your skin like that. Listen, I've got an idea.

(She whispers in **PATTY***'s ear.)*

PATTY. No, come on.

DAWN. Seriously, it really works. It's like a great massage, only much cheaper. What do you say? Let's dump Ashley and Peaches and go for it. It's almost time to leave anyway.

PATTY. Oh, what the hell.

(lights out)

Scene Fourteen
Patty and Dawn at the HHH

(The Hollyhock Hideaway Hotel. **DAWN** *enters in darkness. She flips on a light and throws keys on a bedside table. She falls on the bed on her back and kicks off her heels.* **PATTY** *stands in the doorway.)*

DAWN. Well? Don't just stand there. Come on in.

*(**PATTY** enters awkwardly.)*

Sit down. Relax.

*(**PATTY** goes to the bed and sits on the edge.* **DAWN** *rummages through her purse and pulls out a roll of quarters.)*

Ta da.

(She shows the roll to **PATTY**. *She scoots up on the bed.)*

Come on over. Come on. This is what we came here for, Patty.

*(**DAWN** starts up the magic fingers. They shake as if the bed is vibrating.)*

Mmmm. Feels good, doesn't it? Lie back. Lie back. It's better if you lie back.

*(**DAWN** pushes **PATTY** down. They vibrate in silence for a while.* **DAWN** *rolls on top of* **PATTY** *and begins kissing her.* **PATTY** *throws* **DAWN** *off and jumps off the bed.)*

PATTY. Dawn! My god! What are you doing? I mean, I'm sorry, Dawn. I'm not that way. I guess I didn't make that clear.

DAWN. No, no. You made it clear. You like lumberjacks.

PATTY. Yes. I guess I do. I like Buzz.

DAWN. Buzz is a nice guy. A super nice guy.

PATTY. Yes he is.

DAWN. OK. It's no problem. C'mon. Let's watch some cable.

*(**PATTY** doesn't move.)*

We already paid for the room. Oh, c'mon, Patty. I get you. You straight girls think lesbians have one thing on our minds. Get over yourself, Patty. I'm not desperate.

PATTY. I'm sorry, Dawn. I guess I have a lot to learn about lesbians. I never really knew one. Not well, anyway. I do like you. I'd like to be friends.

DAWN. Good. Me too. OK?

PATTY. OK. *(She sits.)*

DAWN. See? Nothing has to happen.

(They both lie back.)

We're just relaxing together. Everyone needs to relax.

PATTY. I like to relax.

DAWN. Me, too.

(DAWN leans over and kisses PATTY.)

PATTY. Dawn —

DAWN. What?

PATTY. Well, what about the celibacy rule? Have you forgotten about that?

DAWN. It doesn't count as sex if it's two women, Patty. I can't believe you didn't know that.

PATTY. Well, Ashley said —

DAWN. Ashley! Ashley is such a fucking Moonie, Patty. Don't listen to her. Listen, I'm the lesbian and, believe me, it doesn't count.

(They both lie back. DAWN reaches over and puts her hand on PATTY's thigh.)

PATTY. Dawn!

DAWN. Come on!

PATTY. I thought you said we were friends.

DAWN. We are. Now just shut up and relax. I swear, you're so talkative.

(DAWN goes to kiss PATTY. PATTY pushes her off.)

PATTY. Dawn!

(They stare at each other for a brief moment, then PATTY pulls DAWN on top of her. Lights fade out. Pause.)

(Lights back up on DAWN and PATTY in bed. DAWN is sleeping. PATTY sits up and composes a letter aloud.)

PATTY. *(cont.)* Dear Mom,

Big Bone is great. All the secretaries are really wonderful, especially my boss. One of them just gave me my
first orgasm at a fuck motel.

*(She pauses, realizing what she has said. She tries
again.)*

Dear Mom,

Sorry I haven't written. Who has time? I'm trying to
decode a clicking and giggling language and...

(pause)

Dear Mom,

Everything is great. I miss you.

Love, Patty. P.S. Everyone loves your pins.

(lights out)

Scene Fifteen
Patty and Dawn. The Morning After

*(The next day. In the office. The sign reads: 28 ACCI-
DENT-FREE DAYS.* **DAWN** *is at her desk.* **PEACHES**
enters.)

DAWN. Morning, Peaches.

PEACHES. Hi, Dawn. You look different. Did you lose
weight?

*(***PATTY*** *enters.)*

DAWN. Hi, Patty.

PATTY. Dawn.

PEACHES. Patty, doesn't Dawn look great? She lost some
weight.

PATTY. Yeah. Great.

DAWN. Get me a coffee, black. Will ya, Peaches?

PEACHES. Sure. Want anything, Patty? I'm going.

PATTY. No thanks, Peaches.

*(***PEACHES*** *exits.)*

DAWN. Patty, I wanted to talk to you first thing.

PATTY. Right. Listen, Dawn, about last night –

DAWN. No. I'm talking about tonight.

PATTY. Tonight?

DAWN. It's two-step night at Choices. A live band and everything. We've got to get there early, 'cause it's always
packed. And then I thought that afterwards we could –

*(***ASHLEY*** *enters.)*

Ten hut!

ASHLEY. Good one, Dawn! Good morning, Patty! Dawn,
you look truly gorgeous today. Did you lose weight?

DAWN. No.

ASHLEY. I bet you did. You should look at yourself. You're
having a good hair day, too. Enjoy it while it lasts.
(marches into **SUSAN**'s *office)*

PATTY. Look. Dawn. Last night was OK and everything, but –

DAWN. You didn't say anything to Ashley, did you?

PATTY. No. Why?

DAWN. Good. We shouldn't say anything to her. The last thing we want is Ashley to find out about us.

PATTY. Us? Dawn, we've got to have a little talk.

DAWN. We should talk later at Choices. It's safer.

PATTY. Relax. God, Dawn, you're the lesbian, remember? Stop being so paranoid.

DAWN. I'm serious, Patty. Don't say anything to Ashley. OK?

PATTY. To be honest, Dawn, it's not the kind of thing I'd go around bragging about. I mean, I think I'm basically straight.

DAWN. So you're not gonna talk about it?

PATTY. We really need to talk.

(*PEACHES enters.*)

PEACHES. Coffee black. Is everything all right?

DAWN. Patty wants an herbal tea, Peaches.

PEACHES. You're welcome, Dawn. Why didn't you just say so before, Patty?

PATTY. I'm sorry, Peaches. Do you mind?

(*PEACHES stomps off. Clearly, they are trying her patience.*)

DAWN. OK, so later? Pick you up at seven?

PATTY. I already have a date. With Buzz.

DAWN. OK then, more like ten or eleven?

PATTY. Dawn. Listen to me. I – I'm trying to tell you that – that I like lumberjacks.

DAWN. OK, Patty. Don't worry. I'm not the jealous type.

(*DAWN goes to touch PATTY's hair. PATTY pushes DAWN's hand away.*)

PATTY. Dawn!

DAWN. Shit, Patty. You're right. We've got to concentrate really hard on not touching each other when we're in the office. Let's try and keep our hands to ourselves.

(ASHLEY appears in SUSAN's doorway.)

ASHLEY. Not interrupting anything important, I hope.

DAWN. Ashley, are you OK?

ASHLEY. What?

DAWN. I don't know. You've got brown stuff all over your nose.

ASHLEY. Patty. Your girlfriend has a mouth on her.

PATTY. She's not –

(SUSAN comes out of her office.)

SUSAN. Dawn, what are you working on?

DAWN. I – uh –

SUSAN. Get cracking on the charts for that Annual Report. We'll need them for that meeting tomorrow. Patty?

PATTY. Oh. I – uh –

DAWN. She's helping me with –

SUSAN. Mr. Kembunkscher wants a girl with steno upstairs. You know where his office is?

PATTY. *(collecting her steno pad)* Yes.

SUSAN. Good. Let's not lose our heads now, ladies. These next few days are crucial. *(She goes back into her office.)*

DAWN. See you later, Patty.

(DAWN gives PATTY a wink. PATTY quickly exits.)

(to ASHLEY) What're you looking at?

ASHLEY. Nothing.

(PEACHES enters.)

PEACHES. Here you go, Patty. Patty? Hey. Where's Patty?

(blackout)

Scene Sixteen
Susan and Dawn

(The office, later that night. **DAWN** *is sitting in the office, alone.)*

DAWN. FUCK. FUCK. FUCK THIS FUCKING FUCK OF A FUCKER!!! *(She starts pounding on her computer.)*

SUSAN. *(over the intercom)* Dawn?

DAWN. This bastard just froze on me in the middle of the goddamn fucking pie chart. FUCKER!!!

SUSAN. *(coming out of her office)* Dawn. Stop it. Now.

DAWN. Not now, Susan. This fucker is frozen.

*(***SUSAN*** *walks over to* **DAWN** *and turns off her computer.)*

My pie charts!

SUSAN. I'm sure you didn't lose much. You were saving it as you went along, weren't you?

DAWN. *(lying)* Yeah.

SUSAN. Better to work on it tomorrow, when you're feeling fresh. We both know what happens to office machinery when Dawn Midnight gets tired and loses her temper, don't we? Go home, Dawn. Try to get some rest. It's been a long day and you look – actually, you look very different somehow. Is that new eye shadow?

DAWN. No.

*(***SUSAN*** *approaches* **DAWN** *and stares into her face.)*

SUSAN. Mmmm. Something in your eyes…your beautiful, dark eyes.

DAWN. Yours, too.

(pause)

SUSAN. Don't. Let's not.

DAWN. They're beautiful.

SUSAN. No. They're not.

DAWN. You know they are.

SUSAN. Dawn, you're embarrassing me. I'm – I'm not that way. *(losing control)* You're such a lesbian, Dawn. It's why I can't sit next to you in the club meetings. It's why I go insane during that time of the month. I find it hard not to –

(DAWN and SUSAN kiss. SUSAN pulls away.)

DAWN. Don't stop, Susan.

SUSAN. I have to, Dawn. If I don't, I'll –

DAWN. What? You'll what?

SUSAN. I'll crash, Dawn. I swear. I'll break over you like a tidal wave.

(They kiss again.)

DAWN. Tsunami.

(They kiss more. DAWN starts to go down on SUSAN, but SUSAN pulls her back up. SUSAN kneels, hikes up DAWN's skirt and buries her face between DAWN's legs. DAWN moans in ecstasy, then screams in pain.)

You bit me! Jesus H. Christ! You fucking bit me!

(SUSAN stands and turns toward the audience. She wipes a little blood off her mouth.)

SUSAN. Oh, Dawn. I just remembered the celibacy rule.

DAWN. What?

SUSAN. Celibacy. Meaning celibacy. No sex. None. Nada. Nunca. That means no checking into the Hollyhock Hotel with the new recruit.

DAWN. Ashley is fucking dead meat!

SUSAN. Ashley? Ashley? Ashley has nothing to do with this. You don't make a move I don't know about. You don't have a thought I don't already know. Dawn Midnight just can't get enough of straight pussy, can she? If it's straight or better yet married, you just have to fuck it. Well, don't fuck with me, Dawn. Don't fuck with my rules. DON'T FUCK, PERIOD. End of discussion.

(DAWN gathers her things and hobbles toward the door. SUSAN pulls herself together.)

SUSAN. *(cont.)* Dawn? I hope you know how much I love you. I make these rules for a reason.

DAWN. Yeah. Thanks. Thanks, Susan.

SUSAN. Sleep tight. I'll see you in the morning.

(**DAWN** *exits.* **SUSAN** *licks the blood off her fingers. Lights out.*)

Scene Seventeen
In the Car

(Later that night. SUSAN *and* PATTY *are in* SUSAN*'s convertible.* PATTY *is in her pajamas and slippers.* SUSAN *is driving.)*

PATTY. Susan, are you mad at me?

SUSAN. Mad? Why would I be mad? Light me a cigarette, will you? Patty?

PATTY. I – I didn't know you smoked.

SUSAN. There's a lot you don't know about me. I'm a mass of self-destructive habits. Open me up a whiskey sour.

PATTY. What?

SUSAN. There's a cooler in back.

PATTY. *(handing* SUSAN *a whiskey-sour-in-a-can)* You shouldn't drink and drive.

SUSAN. Right. Slide over.

(They switch places while the car is still in motion.)

You drive for a while. Take Route 253.

PATTY. Are you sure? It's so dark and –

*(*SUSAN *pulls the wheel; the car makes a squealing turn.)*

SUSAN. I'm sorry I pulled you out of bed in the middle of the night. I just couldn't sleep. Driving helps me relax.

PATTY. I couldn't sleep either. There's so much tension in the office.

SUSAN. Is there?

PATTY. I guess with the Annual Report and the big meeting tomorrow.

SUSAN. That must be it.

PATTY. Not to mention everyone is PMS. Talk about every man's nightmare. Mr. Kembunkscher –

SUSAN. Don't get me started on him. If Ron Kembunkscher thinks I'm going to fire Peaches Martin, he's got another thing coming.

PATTY. Peaches is getting fired?

SUSAN. Take it easy, Patty. Kembunkscher and I have been over this a million times. I always win. Anyway, you know what they say about men. Angels in the bedroom, devils in the board room. Or is it the other way around?

(SUSAN *laughs. She slips off a high heel and puts her foot over* PATTY*'s on the gas pedal.*)

Come on, Patty. I happen to know this car goes a lot faster.

PATTY. Susan.

SUSAN. Eyes on the road.

PATTY. Don't. It's too fast.

SUSAN. You can handle it, Patty. Breathe. Breathe, Patty. The difference between fear and exhilaration is a deep breath.

PATTY. I can't.

SUSAN. Yes, you can. Keep breathing, Patty.

PATTY. *(taking a deep breath)* Oh, god.

SUSAN. Your life is like this car, Patty. Fully loaded with a big, powerful engine under the hood. It's your choice. You can play it safe or you can open her up and live dangerously. Now, take Buzz Benikee. What would you say Buzz is? About fifty-five? Strictly legal. Now, sleeping with Dawn. That was an adventure, wasn't it?

PATTY. Dawn and I never –

SUSAN. Don't lie about it. Ashley told me. It's OK. I'm not mad at you, Patty. What was it like sleeping with Dawn? *(She presses down the pedal.)* Eighty – eighty-five – ninety miles an hour –

PATTY. Susan, please!

SUSAN. – on a straightaway. It makes you feel heady, all that speed, but you still see what's coming down the road. Now, take me, Patty. I'm a different animal altogether. I can show you how to take curves at top speed.

PATTY. Susan, please.

SUSAN. Breathe, Patty.

(PATTY *breathes.*)

There's no such thing as driving with me, Patty. I am the road. I am the car. I inhabit everything. The whole map is in my bones. And I think you're just like me, Patty. Aren't you? You're just like me. Keep breathing. Keep breathing and feel the road.

(*She stands up and laughs.*)

PATTY. Susan! Susan! Noooooooo!

(*The sound of the car squealing to a halt and hitting something. The bloody carcass of a wombat appears onstage.*)

SUSAN. What was that?

PATTY. A wombat, I think? Is that possible?

SUSAN. Poor thing. Must've escaped from the Cooney Conservation Center.

PATTY. I better take a look.

(PATTY *gets out and looks under the car.* SUSAN *watches her in the rearview mirror.*)

It's still alive. (*She opens the trunk.*) You don't have a gun?

SUSAN. I detest guns. What are you going to do?

(PATTY *removes a tire iron and takes a swipe in the air.*)

Oh, I can't watch.

PATTY. (*coaxing the wombat out from under the car*) Come here. Come here little fella. Come on now. That's a good fella.

(PATTY *beats the wombat to death with the tire iron.* SUSAN *watches.* PATTY *gets so into it that* SUSAN *has to stop her.*)

SUSAN. That's enough, Patty. It's dead.

PATTY. I just hate to see anything suffer.

(*Sound and light cue.* PATTY*'s freak-out wombat-induced hallucination begins.* ASHLEY, DAWN *and* PEACHES *enter with branches.*)

ASHLEY, DAWN & PEACHES. Run Patty Run. Run Patty Run.

(PATTY *begins to fake-run as* ASHLEY, DAWN *and* PEACHES *hit her with the branches.*)

Dusty Woody Chip…Run Patty Run

(*in fake echoey tones*)

ASHLEY. Accident of course – course, course, course…

DAWN. Dragged off by a big cat – cat, cat, cat…

PEACHES. His wife, widow, whatever – ever, ever, ever…

ASHLEY. It's "Reckoning" by Don LeBon – Bon, Bon, Bon…

DAWN. Have another Zima – Zima, Zima, Zima…

PEACHES. Want anything from the water cooler – ooler, ooler, ooler…

ASHLEY, DAWN & PEACHES. (*overlapping each other*)
Twenty-nine days
I'm sure you'll sync up soon.

(PATTY *screams and collapses.* ASHLEY, DAWN *and* PEACHES *disappear.*)

SUSAN. Is something wrong, Patty?

PATTY. I'm just so emotional.

SUSAN. Maybe it's just that time of the month.

PATTY. No, I'm not due for another… (*reaching into her underwear to check*) I'm early!

SUSAN. I'd better take you home, Patty. We have a big day tomorrow.

(*blackout*)

Scene Eighteen
Shit Hits the Fan

(The office. The sign reads: 29 ACCIDENT-FREE DAYS. The desks are gathered into the middle of the office. PEACHES is huddled among them eating a tuna sandwich. ASHLEY enters, discovers the Woman of Steel statue in the trash can and goes into SUSAN's office. MR. KEMBUNKSCHER's voice comes over the P.A.)

MR. KEMBUNKSCHER. *(V.O.)* Miss Martin, could you please come into my office?

PEACHES. Fuck you.

MR. KEMBUNKSCHER. *(V.O.)* Miss Martin, get your size-four-teen butt into my office now!

PEACHES. Fat pig! Fat pig!

MR. KEMBUNKSCHER. *(V.O.)* Hey! I'm waiting for that Annual Report!

PEACHES. Shut up! Shut up! I'm eating my lunch! Baldy ass.

MR. KEMBUNKSCHER. *(V.O.)* Is there anybody out there? Will someone out there tell me what's going on! I want my report! I want my report!

(PATTY enters. PEACHES pops up with a mouthful of sandwich.)

PEACHES. Patty!

(PATTY slaps PEACHES and the sandwich goes flying. PEACHES decks PATTY and retrieves her sandwich.)

That's my lunch!

(DAWN enters wearing sunglasses and carrying a beer in a paper bag.)

DAWN. Sorry I'm late. What gives?

PEACHES. *(simultaneously with PATTY)* I was eating lunch.

PATTY. *(simultaneously with PEACHES)* Peaches hit me.

MR. KEMBUNKSCHER. *(V.O.)* I'm waiting. I'm waiting.

DAWN. Oh crap. *(She goes to her computer.)*

PATTY. *(speaking into the intercom)* Just a minute, Mr. K., I'll take care of it. *(to DAWN)* Dawn! Where have you been?

PEACHES. He wants it in Japanese. I can't even print in American.

PATTY. Jesus.

DAWN. Somebody's been in my hard drive. Oh great, Peaches. My Jeopardy's been erased.

PEACHES. I don't even have a hard drive anymore.

DAWN. Shit, I can't retrieve a thing.

(ASHLEY *reenters. She's holding the crumpled* Woman of Steel *statue and a bottle of toner. She's got black marks around her mouth.*)

PATTY. Ashley, what's your password?

ASHLEY. It's a secret. If I tell you I'll have to kill you.

PATTY. Come on, Ashley. Kembunkscher's on the warpath. *(sees the toner)* Hey, that stuff is toxic.

DAWN. Ashley...gimme the toner.

ASHLEY. Sure, Dawn.

(*She eats the rest of the toner and tosses the bottle to* DAWN.)

You better order more. We're almost out.

PATTY. What are you doing?

ASHLEY. You stay the fuck away from my job. I'm next in line, got it? You've got a pink sweater but if you want a lumberjack jacket, Patty, well then you've got to earn it.

DAWN. Leave her alone, Ashley.

ASHLEY. Aw, isn't love sweet.

MR. KEMBUNKSCHER. *(V.O.)* Hello? Hello? Is this thing working?

PEACHES. I'm having my lunch, you fat pig. You know, lunch? What people eat to live. I'm eating my lunch, you dumb fuck. Leave me alone!

DAWN. Oh, shut up, Peaches!

PEACHES. Don't tell me to shut up! I starve myself and look at me, I'm fat. Patty eats whatever she wants whenever she wants to. She eats a dinner! She eats a dinner!

PATTY. I'm sorry.

PEACHES. Yeah, you're sorry and I'm fat.

ASHLEY. Stop saying that word!!!

PEACHES. FAT! FAT! FAT! How do you like that, you stupid anorexic?

ASHLEY. What?

PEACHES. I read about you in *Mirabella*. You think you're fat but really you're skinny.

ASHLEY. Shut your mouth, Peaches. You don't know what the fuck you're talking about.

PATTY. You guys!

PEACHES. I might not. I just know what I read in a national women's magazine, that's all.

PATTY. The report!

DAWN. Oh, fuck Kembunkscher, Patty! You fuck everybody anyway!

ASHLEY. *(to PEACHES)* If you don't shut your fat trap this minute, I'm going to come over there and shut it for you, you whore!

PEACHES. *(referring to PATTY)* I don't think I'm really the whore in this room, but you can call me that if you like.

PATTY. Shut up, everyone! Just stop talking for one minute please. We're all in a lot of trouble and we only make it worse by fighting.

(SUSAN breezes in with shopping bags.)

ASHLEY, DAWN, PEACHES & PATTY. Susan!

PATTY. *(simultaneously with PEACHES)* Mr. Kembunkscher wants the Annual Report and Ashley won't give me her password.

PEACHES. *(simultaneously with PATTY)* I just wanted a sandwich. It's a healthy sandwich.

MR. KEMBUNKSCHER. *(V.O.)* That's it. I'm coming out there.

SUSAN. *(talking to* MR. KEMBUNKSCHER *on the intercom)* Everything's fine, Ron. I'll have that report right to you. *(furious)* What happened, Patty? I thought I left you in charge here. *(sits at a computer and snaps into action)* Ashley's password is "Hello Kitty." Dawn, take over and print. Peaches, take your little baggy of food and we'll go into my office and –

ASHLEY. Oh, here comes the almighty Woman of Steel. She's going to solve all the problems. She doesn't care that her perfect, pretty, little Patty Johnson is porking Buzz at the Hollyhock Hideaway Humping Hole.

SUSAN. Patty, get Ashley over to Cooney General.

ASHLEY. *(brandishing an empty water cooler jug and menacing* PATTY*)* Not so fast, you butt-licking, ladder-climbing, little bitch. You're in way over your head.

DAWN & PEACHES. Ashley, stop.

SUSAN. Ashley, drop it.

ASHLEY. No, why should I? Why should Patty get everything and we get nothing? Patty never killed for you, Susan.

DAWN. Jesus, Ashley! What do you want us all to go to jail and get raped by a stick?

PEACHES. Apparently. Apparently she does.

PATTY. Ashley, I don't want to fight.

ASHLEY. Then you better run. You better run, little girl.

(A big hair-pulling cat fight ensues. In the course of it, PATTY *accidentally turns off the switch that controls the mill. Siren and lights, general chaos.)*

SUSAN. All right everyone, calm down. I can handle Kembunkscher. Dawn, get Ashley to emergency and get a lock and key on that toner. She's had one too many toner shakes this year. Peaches, to the ladies' room. I think you know the right thing to do. Patty, can you make sure you get to the meeting on time this evening?

PATTY. Yes.

SUSAN. And, Patty, take a shower. You stink of lumberjack.

(blackout)

Scene Nineteen
Guts/Prep

(The office. Later that day. **ASHLEY, PEACHES, PATTY**
and **DAWN** *are waiting for* **SUSAN** *to arrive and start the*
BOW meeting. There is a moment of tense silence.)

PEACHES. Patty, I told you not to pull the switch.

*(***SUSAN** *enters.)*

How'd it go with Mr. Kembunkscher, Susan?

SUSAN. It went fine.

PEACHES. *(nervously running off at the mouth)* Oh, that's good.
Because I thought Patty was going to get fired the way
she pulled that switch. I mean, I warned her, Susan.
The day she came here I told her, "Whatever you do,
Patty, don't pull that switch." Because I have done it
and I know. It's very, very bad when it happens…

SUSAN. No, Peaches. Patty is not getting fired. Ron and I
have decided to let you go.

PEACHES. What?

SUSAN. Just kidding. Come here, Peaches. Look at you.
What am I going to do with you? You had to stuff your
face, didn't you? You couldn't get along on a shake
like the rest of us. Isn't Patty helping you?

PEACHES. Susan, I was really hungry.

SUSAN. You were overeating, Peaches. That's a mental
disorder. I can help you, but you've got to meet me
halfway.

PEACHES. I'm trying, Susan. I'm trying so hard.

SUSAN. You know, Peaches, when I picked you out from that
crop of cows down at Big Bone Beverage, I thought
I was doing you a favor. But now I see I was wrong.
There's nothing inside you. Nothing worth redeem-
ing or saving. You're weak. You're pathetic to look at.
Your fat ass is the symptom, Peaches, not the problem.
Nothing ever changes with you.

(Taking out photocopies of **PEACHES**'s *behind and passing them out to everyone)*

SUSAN. *(cont.)* December '91. No change. April '93. No change. Last month, Peaches. No change. Bend over, Peaches. We want an update.

PATTY. That's enough, Susan.

SUSAN. Oh, poor Patty Johnson can't stand to see anything suffer.

PATTY. Peaches, sit down.

PEACHES. It's OK, Patty.

PATTY. It's not OK. None of this is OK.

SUSAN. Do what Patty says, Peaches.

DAWN. Patty, are you PMS?

PATTY. What are you doing, Susan?

SUSAN. What am I doing?

PATTY. I'm not stupid. I notice things.

SUSAN. What things, Patty?

PATTY. Like every girl has a jacket. A lumberjack jacket.

SUSAN. They're nice jackets aren't they? Good and warm. Better made than a woman's coat. Have you ever noticed that, Patty? How men's clothes are better made than women's and usually half as expensive? It's a crime. A while ago, before you came on, we decided to rectify this crime. We decided we wanted good jackets, too. It gets cold in winter. Only the lumberjacks won't give us their jackets, so we take them.

(PATTY *tries to bolt.* **ASHLEY** *and* **DAWN** *grab her and force her to her knees, facing the audience.)*

PATTY. You kill them, don't you! You kill the lumberjacks!

SUSAN. Don't act so surprised, Patty. Don't tell me the idea hasn't crossed your mind. How do you think we got to be so self-possessed and strong? From drinking Slim-Fast?

PATTY. You won't get away with this. I'm calling the police.

(SUSAN *picks up the phone and hands it to* **PATTY**.)

SUSAN. You might want to call Buzz first.

PATTY. What?

SUSAN. He's on your speed dial, isn't he?

PATTY. What are you talking about, Susan?

SUSAN. We put the bull's-eye on your little Buzz.

PATTY. What the fuck?

SUSAN. It only makes sense, Patty. He's around a lot. He's off guard. It's perfect. Tonight you'll go to the Breezy Barn, as usual. Ask him to play a song for you on the jukebox. While he's away from the table, you'll slip a tablet into his drink –

PATTY. He loves me.

SUSAN. I love you. Peaches, Ashley, Dawn – we love you. Buzz doesn't love you. He loves an idea of you. I even love the killer in you. Now that's love.

PATTY. I'm not a killer!

SUSAN. But you're so good at everything. Everything you try you excel at.

PATTY. Why Buzz? Buzz never hurt anyone. Why not one of the others? Why not Hank or Sandy – the way he's always pawing at the girls –

SUSAN. We don't kill them because they're bad. We kill them because we're bad.

PATTY. This is insane. This can't be happening. Dawn, please.

(PATTY *grabs* DAWN. DAWN *takes* PATTY's *hand off of her.*)

DAWN. Don't touch me, Patty.

PATTY. Ashley? (*quickly realizes* ASHLEY *is a dead end*) Peaches, how could you do this?

PEACHES. I don't know, Patty. It's fun. There's food. We can eat. There's pizza and ice cream and Kahlua and you can mix them together. And it's dark, Patty. And we yell. A sound comes out of my mouth, huge, like I never could have imagined.

SUSAN. Peaches is the star of our kill nights. Aren't you, Peaches? Stop tormenting yourself, Patty. I hate to see your beautiful face all screwed up.

PATTY. Don't you tell me about beautiful! I thought you were beautiful! I thought you were the most beautiful woman I'd ever seen in my life! But now I see – you're ugly! Ugly! Ugly!

SUSAN. You're right, Patty. I am ugly.

PATTY. Well, I'm not! I'm not ugly. I'm pretty! Everyone says so. Buzz says so. He tells me all the time. Dawn said I have a great body. I was homecoming queen. I'm pretty! I'm pretty!

SUSAN. All right. You're pretty. Now what? What do you do now? Go back home? Back to Mom and Dad? Back to Piney Bluff, Oregon? Look – you can have your old room back. It's just how you left it – your pom-poms on the bureau and a snapshot of you and your girl-friends at the Sadie Hawkins dance tacked up on the wall. How sweet. Won't Mom and Dad be happy to see you? I guess Dad was right after all. You should stick close to home so he can keep an eye on you. Then what'll you do? Date some of the local boys till you meet Mr. Good Enough after a long string of Saturday night blow jobs in the front seat? Oh, Patty Johnson is very popular. She's liberated. She's good for a blow job but she won't swallow –

PATTY. Fuck you – you cunt whore bitch!

(**PATTY** *stabs* **SUSAN** *with a phone message spike. The girls all rush to* **PATTY**.)

SUSAN. NOOO! Leave us.

(**ASHLEY**, **DAWN** *and* **PEACHES** *exit.* **SUSAN** *pulls the message spike out of her shoulder.*)

Christ! *(She takes one of the messages off the spike.)* What do you have to do to get your messages around here? Ow, Patty, that smarts.

PATTY. I'm sorry, Susan.

SUSAN. Good girls don't stab people, Patty. Nice aim, or were you going for my heart?

PATTY. You made me do it.

SUSAN. You wanted to do it. You loved it, didn't you? Admit it, Patty. Look at yourself. Look at you.

PATTY. Yes! I am. I am what you say.

SUSAN. You never liked Peaches, did you? You just pretended to like her.

PATTY. Yes, yes.

SUSAN. Dawn was your toy, wasn't she?

PATTY. Yes, I used her.

SUSAN. And you wanted Ashley to die, didn't you?

PATTY. Yes, I loathe her. I despise her.

SUSAN. And Buzz is a lousy fuck, isn't he?

PATTY. Yes, yes, the bastard!

SUSAN. But most of all, you hate me. Isn't that right, Patty?

PATTY. Yes! Yes! I hate you. I hate you.

(PATTY *lunges at* SUSAN, *then collapses in her lap, crying.*)

SUSAN. I know, Patty. I know. Some days I wish I was still that lonely receptionist eating shit every day for lunch and dreaming my life away inside the pages of a catalog. Everything changes so fast.

(PATTY *has no more fight left. She's crossed over.*)

PATTY. What, what do we use, to do it?

SUSAN. Well, that depends on the girl. Some like to take advantage of their Cooney firearms. Some prefer the hands-on approach. Either way it comes down to the chain saw.

PATTY. The same one they use to kill the trees?

SUSAN. That's right.

PATTY. It's poetic, isn't it?

SUSAN. If you like.

PATTY. *(referring to* **SUSAN***'s wounded shoulder)* Let me help you.

SUSAN. I'm fine.

PATTY. No, you're not. I see someone, behind the facade. Someone who hurts and needs. What happened to you, Susan?

SUSAN. OK. My story goes like this. I was born and then I was fucked over and fucked over and fucked over so many times that I can't separate it out anymore. I've lived all over. I did everything. I held up liquor stores. I lived on stolen credit cards. The FBI is after me. Susan Curtis is not my real name. Whatever friends and family I once had I've left behind long ago. I can't let anyone close. It's too risky. Funny, all the high-speed car chases and the aliases. But some things are just too risky. There, is that enough for you, Patty, or too much?

PATTY. I'm sorry Susan, I didn't mean to make you feel –

SUSAN. That's all for now, Patty. Go home and get ready. I want you to look extra pretty for him tonight.

PATTY. I know just what to wear.

(lights out)

Scene Twenty
Kill Night

*(The office. Later that night. Hypnotic drum music.
SUSAN sits center, facing the audience. PEACHES and
ASHLEY, wearing their hunting jackets and hats, stand
at attention behind her. During the course of this scene,
the office walls give way to reveal a ritual clearing in a
towering wood, illuminated by the light of a full moon.)*

SUSAN. Number 10?

PEACHES. Crank up his chain saw. Wave it over his head!

SUSAN. Number 6?

PEACHES. Take his pants away. Dress him in panty hose.

SUSAN. Number 29?

PEACHES. Charge expensive items on his AmEx Card using
his cellular phone while he listens helplessly!

SUSAN. Number 48?

PEACHES. Tie him to the ground, spread-eagle, and stamp
the ground between his legs.

SUSAN. Number 69?

PEACHES. Refuse all offers of marriage!

SUSAN. We rendezvous with Patty and our subject at Pokey
Point in twenty minutes. Let's freshen our lipstick and
head out.

(SUSAN exits.)

PEACHES & ASHLEY. *(in cheerleader cadence)*
Kill night! Yeah, yeah, yeah
Kill night! Go, go, go
Kill night!

*(The clearing. Midnight. Van Halen guitar music plays
super loud. The stage is littered with the trappings of a
glutinous bacchanalia. liquor bottles, pizza boxes, ice
cream cartons, etc. PEACHES and ASHLEY are stuffing
their faces with pizza and cake, chugging Jagermeister
and screaming drunkenly. They are wearing wacky,*

slutty lingerie. **PEACHES** *is covered in blood.* **PATTY** *enters, also dressed in slutty lingerie, carrying a bottle of crème de menthe. She is hysterical, alternately giggling and sobbing and swigging from the bottle. Offstage,* **BUZZ** *yells for* **PATTY***, and they all freeze. He crosses the stage behind them, stumbling and calling for* **PATTY***. As he exits, the others unfreeze and resume screaming and eating. We hear the sounds of a chain saw and* **BUZZ** *screaming.)*

ASHLEY. Patty! Get on Buzz's cellular and order us some more pizzas.

PEACHES. Yeah, and bread sticks. Get those bread sticks. They are good!

(The loud sound of a chain saw.)

BUZZ. *(offstage)* Oh god! What do you want from me!!

*(***PATTY** *is having a hard time keeping her cool.)*

ASHLEY & PEACHES. *(together, mocking* **BUZZ***)* "What do you want from me!!"

*(***ASHLEY** *and* **PEACHES** *laugh.* **DAWN** *enters. There is blood all over her hands and on her mouth and chin.)*

DAWN. Help me! Help me, you guys! This blood is gonna get on my outfit!

ASHLEY. Geez. What? Did you hit an artery or something?

PEACHES. How's it going, Dawn?

DAWN. Oh, god, it's great! You should see him. What's left of him. Thanks, Peaches. You hardly left us anything.

*(***PATTY** *scampers off.)*

Susan is amazing. She's really on tonight. That reminds me, Ashley. I'm supposed to tell you you're next.

*(***ASHLEY** *rubs her hands together and heads off in the direction of* **BUZZ***.)*

PEACHES & DAWN. *(together, chanting)* Kill the pig! Kill the pig! *(They laugh.)*

DAWN. Hey, is there more pizza?

PEACHES. Patty, did you order more – Patty?

(They see she is missing.)

She was just here a minute ago.

DAWN. Maybe she's peeing.

PEACHES. Nope, the toilet paper's still here. Shit, Dawn. I hope she's not having a fucking freak attack. We better find her before Susan finds out!

(**PATTY** *appears upstage, looking disheveled and completely insane. She has gone off the deep end and is wielding an ax.*)

PATTY. Oh, Susan's gonna find out, all right. She's gonna find out the hard way. *(She swings the ax.)*

PEACHES. Patty!

DAWN. Peaches, stay back! Patty! It's OK. You're just a little delirious from too much pizza. Put down the ax, OK?

(sounds of the chain saw and **BUZZ** *screaming)*

PATTY. *(collapsing in horror)* Buzz!

PEACHES. She looks a little wan, doesn't she?

(**ASHLEY** *enters ecstatic and covered in blood.*)

ASHLEY. You guys! Help me!

(Nobody does. **ASHLEY** *towels off.)*

Patty – your go!

DAWN. Ashley, she's freaking.

ASHLEY. I knew she didn't have it in her.

PEACHES. It's really not so hard once you try it, Patty. *(moves toward* **PATTY**)

PATTY. Get away from me!

DAWN. Come on, Patty. It's us! It's your friends.

PATTY. You just stay away!

ASHLEY. You're not gonna spoil this for me, Patty. I've prepared too long and hard for this night.

(**ASHLEY** *goes to* **PATTY**. **PATTY** *swings the ax.*)

Baby!

PATTY. Stay away from me! I'll kill you. I'll kill you first.

DAWN. God, Patty, get a grip.

ASHLEY. Really.

PEACHES. Is she for real?

PATTY. You're damn right I am, Peaches, you moron. Anyone comes within three feet of me gets this ax in their head. Got it?

PEACHES. OK, but you're really spoiling this whole thing, you know.

DAWN. Someone get Susan.

PATTY. No! No Susan! I'm getting in the Trooper and I'm getting out of here.

(SUSAN *enters, wearing a white bra and panties. She is covered with blood.*)

SUSAN. Where are you going, Patty?

PATTY. Out of here. Out of these woods. Don't worry, Susan. I won't tell anyone. I just want out.

SUSAN. Put down that ax. It's not a toy.

PATTY. No! I just want to go home, Susan. I just want things to be like they were.

SUSAN. They'll never be like they were, Patty. I won't be able to keep you on at Cooney. You know that. Now give me the ax. You're tired. You need to rest.

PATTY. Susan, stay away from me. Please.

SUSAN. Are you going to put that ax through my pretty hairdo?

PATTY. No. I'd never be able to kill you, Susan. You're right. Things will never be the same.

(PATTY *puts her head on a stump and tries to cut it off with the ax. All rush to stop her.*)

SUSAN. (*holding* PATTY) Help! Somebody! Get the Jagermeister. There, there.

DAWN. It's her first time.

PEACHES. She's afraid she won't get it right. Dawn was afraid her first time, too. Remember, Dawn?

ASHLEY. She can't do it. She can't stomach it.

PEACHES. I'll help you, Patty. I'll hold the saw while you direct it –

SUSAN. Peaches! Patty's going to be fine. She's just a little afraid, that's all. Remember what I always told you. aim high – if you fall, you'll only be that much closer to your dreams.

(SUSAN *lets go of* PATTY *who falls in a crumpled heap.*)

What's it gonna be, Patty? What's life gonna be for Patty Johnson?

(*Comatose,* PATTY *gets up. With one last look at* SUSAN, *she walks offstage to the torture stump. We hear the chain saw rev up, then the sound of* BUZZ*'s screams.* ASHLEY, DAWN, PEACHES *and* SUSAN *sing a plaintive, yet heart-warming, rendition of "Kumbaya."* PATTY *enters. She is covered in blood and carrying* BUZZ*'s severed forearm. Her face is a blank. She drops the forearm. The others look at her expectantly.*)

PATTY. You guys! Help me!

(*They all laugh and rush to her, à la Miss America.*)

ASHLEY, DAWN, PEACHES & SUSAN. (*sing-song*)
Patty gets a jacket!
Patty gets a jacket!

(*They giggle and click.* PATTY *giggles and clicks with them.*)

ASHLEY. So. Congratulations, Patty.

PEACHES. Yes, Congratulations, Patty.

(PATTY *turns to* DAWN.)

DAWN. You got what it takes, Patty.

(DAWN *and* PATTY *hug. Then all except* PATTY *freeze.*)

PATTY. (*to audience*) My first Kill Night. It seems so long ago. Susan took it on the lam soon after that. Now, I'm office manager and I love it. I do things differently but, as we say in BOW, it's all in the execution.

(PATTY, SUSAN, ASHLEY, DAWN and PEACHES walk menacingly toward the audience in a V-formation with PATTY in the lead. They chant.)

ALL. Patty's got her jacket now
She fits in with the rest
She cut her boyfriend into bits
And so she passed the test.

Save? No.
We're way beyond saving.

We're at the end. We should provide a moral for this story
But this is not a moral tale or complex allegory
No, we prefer you think of this as purely cautionary
Remember, sitting next to you could be a secretary!

(They all click and giggle. Lights out.)

The End

ABOUT THE FIVE LESBIAN BROTHERS

The Five Lesbian Brothers are Maureen Angelos, Babs Davy, Dominique Dibbell, Peg Healey, and Lisa Kron. The Brothers came together as a theater company in 1989 after performing together in various other combinations at the Obie award–winning WOW Cafe Theatre in New York City's East Village.

Together the Brothers have written five plays, *Voyage to Lesbos* (1990), *Brave Smiles* (1992), *The Secretaries* (1994), *Brides of the Moon* (1996), and *Oedipus at Palm Springs* (2006), which was written by Maureen Angelos, Dominique Dibbell, Peg Healey, and Lisa Kron.

The Brothers' work has been presented Off-Broadway and Off-Off Broadway by New York Theatre Workshop, the Joseph Papp Public Theatre, the WOW Cafe Theatre, Downtown Art Company, Performance Space 122, Dixon Place, La Mama, the Kitchen, and the Whitney Museum of American Art at Phillip Morris. They have toured to London, Los Angeles, San Francisco, San Diego, Houston, Columbus, Seattle, Philadelphia, Boston, and the deep woods of Michigan. Their plays have also been produced by other companies throughout the United States and, believe it or not, in Zagreb, Croatia.

The Brothers are the recipients of a Village Voice Obie Award, a New York Dance and Performance Award ("Bessie"), a GLAAD Media Award, and a New York Press Award as Best Performance Group. An anthology of their plays entitled *Five Lesbian Brothers/Four Plays* was published in 2000 by Theatre Communications Group and was nominated for a Lambda Literary award.

Also by
The Five Lesbian Brothers...

Brave Smiles

Brides of the Moon

Oedipus at Palm Springs

Voyage to Lesbos

OTHER TITLES AVAILABLE FROM SAMUEL FRENCH

OEDIPUS AT PALM SPRINGS

The Five Lesbian Brothers
Maureen Angelos, Babs Davy, Dominique Dibbell,
Peg Healey and Lisa Kron

Comedic Tragedy / 5f

Irreverent theater group The Five Lesbian Brothers get their greasy prints on a classic. *Oedipus at Palm Springs* follows the dark adventure of two couples on a retreat to the desert resort town. While new parents Fran and Con try desperately to jump-start their sex life, May-December love bunnies Prin and Terri can't keep their hands off each other. What begins as a hilarious, boozey weekend takes a horrific turn after a secret is revealed. Two parts comedy with a shot of tragedy shaken over ice, *Oedipus at Palm Springs* is a brave examination of the messy guts of relationships.

"Along the way to the inevitable dark twist is much lightness and enlightenment to revel in–not just a lot of zingy one-liners about commitment, gay life in America, parenthood, and growing older, but also a real sense of these four women as women, friends, and lovers…It may be the saddest comedy you'll ever see.
– *The Boston Globe*

"Richly funny as it is, *Oedipus at Palm Springs* is also a serious inquiry into the unforeseen extremities of despair that can attend the search for a pure and lasting love."
– *The New York Times*

"Sensitive storytelling."
– *New York Magazine*

OTHER TITLES AVAILABLE FROM SAMUEL FRENCH

BRAVE SMILES

The Five Lesbian Brothers
Maureen Angelos, Babs Davy, Dominique Dibbell,
Peg Healey and Lisa Kron

Comedy / 5f

In *Brave Smiles...*Another Lesbian Tragedy, master satirists the Five Lesbian Brothers turn their merciless eyes on the history of lesbians in theater, film, and literature. From their dismal yet erotically charged beginnings at the orphanage under the grip of a sadistic headmistress, our five heroines cross continents and a century to face their absurdly tragic ends. Along the way, they experience alcoholism, suicide, loneliness, pill popping, blacklisting, and a malignant brain tumor. Students of the lesbian art of misery will recognize gleeful skewerings of *The Well of Loneliness, The Group, Maedchen in Uniform,* and *The Children's Hour* in this rollicking, hilarious, and smart multicharacter classic.

"Smart, satirical farce that uses laughter and touches of raunchy humor to debunk the myth of the doomed lesbian."
— *The New York Times*

"Parodies gay clichés about lesbian destiny with deadly accuracy."
—*LA Times*